WITHDRAWN
FOR SALE

For a second speech eluded her, then she said tightly, 'We can't talk here, Lachlan—not in a crowded dance hall.'

'Then let's go somewhere else…' His eyes wandered over her slim figure, seeing the way her dress moulded to every curve and how the apricot colour enhanced her glowing skin. 'My God, Christa—I can't bear this,' he said roughly. 'You look quite…beautiful.' He hesitated, and then said huskily, 'Please…let's have a dance together—just one…'

'That's not a good idea, Lachlan,' she said unsteadily. 'You...you don't need to have a duty dance with me…'

'For God's sake,' he said savagely.

His hand took her bare arm and she shivered, feeling the flickers of desire going through her like a hot knife through butter.

'If you don't trust me—if you really want us to part—think of it as a "last waltz", then. We can't end like this—with no communication at all!'

The words 'we can't end like this' echoed sadly in Christa's ears. She wanted him—oh, how she wanted him—and longed for everything to be as it had been before, when she'd thought he loved her for herself alone…

Just one more time, then… She offered no resistance when he put his arm round her waist and pressed her body fiercely to his.

It was a kind of torture, reminding her of their lovemaking only a few days ago, when his body had locked with hers and they had been as one. He put his cheek to hers and she could smell the scent of soap on him, feel the slight roughness of his chin, his legs against hers as they moved in unison to the beat of the music.

It was as if they were welded together—and it was wonderful and terrible at the same time. Would this really be the last time she would ever be so close to him, feeling his breath on her face, his lips tracing a trail of little kisses down her neck?

Dear Reader

Sometimes our first impressions of people are wrong! I have jumped to conclusions too soon about people I've met in the past, and I thought it would be interesting to explore my heroine's initial response to Lachlan and her gradual understanding of his character because of his past history.

I set this story, as I do many of my books, in Scotland—a place I love—and I hope you like the setting. It was fun to write—I hope you enjoy it too!

Best wishes

Judy

RETURN OF DR MAGUIRE

BY
JUDY CAMPBELL

Published in Great Britain 2014
by Mills & Boon, an imprint of Harlequin (UK) Limited
Large Print edition 2014
Eton House, 18-24 Paradise Road,
Richmond, Surrey, TW9 1SR

ISBN: 978-0-263-23911-9

Harlequin (UK) Limited's policy is to use papers that are natural, renewable and recyclable products and made from wood grown in sustainable forests. The logging and manufacturing processes conform to the legal environmental regulations of the country of origin.

Printed and bound in Great Britain
by CPI Antony Rowe, Chippenham, Wiltshire

Judy Campbell is from Cheshire. As a teenager she spent a great year at high school in Oregon, USA, as an exchange student. She has worked in a variety of jobs, including teaching young children, being a secretary and running a small family business. Her husband comes from a medical family, and one of their three grown-up children is a GP. Any spare time—when she's not writing romantic fiction—is spent playing golf, especially in the Highlands of Scotland.

Recent titles by Judy Campbell:

CELEBRITY IN BRAXTON FALLS
REUNITED: A MIRACLE MARRIAGE
FROM SINGLE MUM TO LADY
HIRED: GP AND WIFE
THE GP'S MARRIAGE WISH

These books are also available in eBook format from www.millsandboon.co.uk

Praise for Judy Campbell:

'Cute, romantic and a hot doctor.
What's not to like?'
—*goodreads.com* on
REUNITED: A MARRIAGE MIRACLE

Dedication

To Donald, patient and long-suffering
when the muse deserts me—
my very own hero!

CHAPTER ONE

'I JUST DO not believe it!' muttered Christa Lennox. 'What the hell is that man doing?'

Titan, the Border terrier, lying at the foot of Christa's desk, sprang up and looked at her enquiringly with head cocked to one side.

'Don't bark, Titan!' she warned him sternly.

She opened the window and leaned forward to get a better view of the opposite wall, squinting through the dancing shadows of the trees nearby. Her gaze was riveted on a man perched precariously at the top of a ladder, hacking away at the guttering and filling a sack suspended from a rung.

Yet another thieving toerag trying to take what he could—and in broad daylight too! Well, she'd darned well show him he wasn't going to get away with it—two burglaries in a fortnight were two too many! On top of the tragedy of dear Isobel dying so suddenly three weeks ago, it was just all too much…

Christa swung away from the surgery window and raced through Reception, closely followed by Titan. She ran towards the ladder at the side of the car park, her auburn hair escaping from its clips and springing out in a mad bob. No point in ringing the police on a Sunday—it would take hours for them to come.

She and Titan skidded to a halt at the bottom of the ladder.

'If you're trying to nick lead from the roof, you're too late—it's all gone!' she yelled up at the man. 'Get down now, or I'll call the police!'

Titan joined in by barking ferociously and adding an extra growl or two for good measure. The man twisted round and looked down, frowning. He had tied a large handkerchief round his lower face so that only his eyes were visible. Trying to remain anonymous, thought Christa scornfully. 'Titan! Titan! Be quiet!' she commanded.

The dog lay down, panting with its tongue lolling out, and watched her adoringly. The man's glance flicked over to Christa, slowly taking in her angry upturned face and sweeping over her indignant figure.

There was a pause before he said rather irritably, 'Well—what is it?'

Christa, put her hands on her hips. 'I want to know what on earth you're doing up there!'

He raised an eyebrow. 'Excuse me?'

'Could you tell me why you're on the roof?'

The man leaned on the ladder, a flash of annoyance in the clear blue eyes that met hers, then whipped the handkerchief from his face, revealing tanned good looks and an irritated expression.

'Not that it's anything to do with you, but I'm examining the guttering—it looks as if it's on its last legs.'

Christa wasn't to be put off. 'Examining the guttering, my foot!' she said angrily. 'Come down now!' she ordered. 'I can't carry on a conversation when you're up there!'

He shrugged, half-amused. 'Oh, for God's sake...of all the bossy women...' He descended the ladder, leaping lightly down the last three rungs, and the little dog sprang up and would have thrown himself at the man's legs if Christa hadn't grabbed his collar.

'Don't worry, Titan—I can handle this…'

Titan sank back unwillingly and Christa turned back to the man and demanded peremptorily, 'Well? What have you got to say for yourself?'

He leaned against the wall in front of her with hands stuffed into his pockets, his eyes narrowed, ranging coolly over her. 'Do you always sound like a headmistress? Now just what's bugging you?'

A moment's doubt—could this guy *really* be a thief? He seemed so assured, so…brazen. Surely a thief would have taken off by now? He stared at her boldly, and she decided that he was just bluffing it out, conning her into thinking he was a legitimate builder.

Christa drew herself up to her full five feet six inches and said majestically, 'I want to know what excuse you've got to give for this daylight robbery—taking a chance because it's a Sunday and the place is empty, I'll bet!'

He laughed out loud and Christa blinked. He

didn't seem a whit worried by her threat to call the police or her accusation—in fact, he looked totally relaxed, in charge of the situation, no sign of being intimidated. She glared at him, looking him straight in the eye, and he stared impudently back at her, making fun of her. The cheeky bastard!

She shouldn't have looked at his eyes—massive error! She was taken aback by their compelling shade of deep, clear blue, fringed with black lashes and...well, they were incredibly unusual...even sexy—which, of course, was nothing to do with the situation whatsoever, she thought irritably.

The man had a tall, spare figure, dressed in faded shorts and a ripped shirt, revealing a muscled torso. He could have got a job playing the lead in a James Bond movie or doing ads for some exotic men's shaving lotion, reflected Christa... And for a split nanosecond she felt an unexpected flutter of excitement somewhere in the region of her stomach.

It took her unawares, made her cross because after her experience with Colin Maitland, she was off all men for a very long time, wasn't she? She crushed the desolate, empty feeling that seemed to be a reflex action whenever she thought of that unmitigated rat, and told herself to stop reacting like a teenager being turned on by some celebrity just because the man in front of her was reasonably good looking.

She cleared her throat and said sternly, 'If you're not pinching lead, who gave you permission to look at the guttering—if that's what you were doing?'

'I don't have to ask anyone's permission—I own the house.'

She stared at him witheringly. 'You *own* the house? Don't be ridiculous! How can it belong to you? Dr Maguire only died three weeks ago and probate can't have been granted yet.'

He said quietly and without apparent emotion, 'Isobel Maguire was my mother. She left me Ardenleigh in her will.'

'Oh, my God…' Christa's hand flew to her mouth, her eyes wide with embarrassment. 'I'm really sorry—I didn't realise…' Her voice faltered, and she gazed at him in a stunned way.

So *this* was the mysterious son, Lachlan, that Isobel had rarely mentioned, and who, as far as she was aware, had never visited his mother…

'Perhaps you should make sure of your facts before making accusations,' the man suggested coldly, an edge of sarcasm to his voice.

'I had no idea who you were. If you'd let us know you were coming I wouldn't have leaped to conclusions when I saw you with a handkerchief over your face on the roof,' she protested, slightly stung that he was putting all the blame on her for not knowing who he was. 'We've had such a spate of burglaries I thought you were yet another thief.'

He nodded rather wearily, pushing his spikily cut thick hair back from his forehead. 'The handkerchief was to protect my lungs from the showers of dirt I was disturbing—but, yes, I guess you're right. I should have told the practice I was coming. It's all been a bit of a rush.'

Her tone softened. 'We knew Isobel had a son, but we had no idea where you lived…'

'I flew in from Australia on Friday and came up from Heathrow yesterday. I stayed in a pub last night, but tonight I'll stay here if there's a habitable room.'

'You couldn't make it to her funeral?'

'No,' he said curtly. 'It was too late by the time I was contacted by her solicitor—I didn't even know she'd died until a few days ago.'

Christa bit her lip. How could she have been so tactless? It was shocking that no one had known how to find him to tell him about his mother. He must feel terrible about that.

'I'm so sorry…' she repeated, and her voice trailed off, but the man had turned his attention back to the building. Christa looked at him more closely. Now she knew who he was, she saw the family resemblance to his mother, who had also been tall and with those clear blue eyes. There was no doubt he had inherited the good looks that ran in the Maguire family.

The man looked sadly at the vast untidy lawn, the dense undergrowth beneath the trees at the end of the garden. 'Everywhere looks very neglected… When I was young the garden was always immaculate, and that little copse well managed. I guess my mother had no interest in the place.'

'She was too busy,' said Christa defensively. 'Isobel's work meant everything to her—and being on her own, of course, it can't have been easy, having to look after everything.'

'I don't suppose it was easy, but frankly it looks as if it's falling down. I can't believe she left it in such a state…'

'I know she kept meaning to have things done. There never seemed to be time…'

'A great pity,' observed the man with some asperity.

He didn't seem to have much sympathy for his mother, reflected Christa, even though Isobel had been alone and had worked so damned hard that it had probably contributed to her death. There was something rather…well, callous about his attitude.

'It may have been that latterly she wasn't feeling very well and hadn't the energy to turn to domestic matters,' suggested Christa rather coldly.

Lachlan nodded. 'Maybe you're right,' he conceded. 'But just look at the state of those windows and woodwork…I used to escape through that window when I was a kid and was about to get a belting for something I'd done—I think it would fall out now if I opened it!' He turned and held out his hand, saying briskly, 'Anyway, it's about time we introduced ourselves. I'm Lachlan Maguire…and you are…?'

'I'm Christa Lennox, and I am…or rather was…your mother's colleague, her junior partner in the practice.'

The expression on Lachlan's face changed subtly from pleasant to wary, the blue eyes widening slightly. He repeated tersely, 'Christa Lennox? You worked with my mother?'

'Why, yes…' Christa looked at Lachlan, puzzled. 'Is there something wrong?'

'No…no, of course not.' Then he added casually after a pause, 'I used to know a man called Angus Lennox—are you a relation, by any chance?'

A look of wry amusement flickered across Christa's face. 'Ah…the black sheep of the family…wicked Uncle Angus,' she remarked. 'How did you know him?'

Lachlan idly kicked a stone away from his foot. 'Oh…he used to come to the house sometimes…' He looked up at Christa, a spark of curiosity in those clear blue eyes. 'And do you know what he did to deserve that reputation?'

Christa shrugged. 'Oh, I don't know all the details and it's a tragic story. I know that he left his wife and child and my father was so outraged by his behaviour he wouldn't speak about him, then Angus was killed in a car crash—a long time ago now.'

Lachlan nodded sombrely. 'I remember that happening…as you say, it was a long time ago.' He smiled. 'Anyway, enough about your wicked uncle—tell me how you came to work with my mother.'

'My own mother was ill some years ago and I was desperate to get a job here as my father had died, and Isobel offered me one. I loved your mother very much—she was a sweet woman and was extremely kind to me over so many things…' Christa's voice faltered slightly and she swallowed hard. 'I was devastated when Isobel collapsed and died so suddenly—I couldn't believe it. It'll be very difficult to find someone to replace her—we shall all miss her so much.'

Lachlan took a rag out of his pocket and wiping his filthy hands remarked, 'You won't have to look far if I take on this place.'

'What do you mean?'

For the first time a fleeting look of sadness crossed Lachlan's strong features. 'My mother left me a letter—you will have known from the post-mortem that her heart had been very damaged, and I think she knew she was on borrowed time. Amongst other things, she wanted me to take over the practice, and it's something I will have to think about very carefully. It's a big decision to make. The house needs such a lot doing to it, and the surgery at the side is rather the worse for wear—it's going to eat up money.'

Christa only heard the first part of his reply and stared at him with her mouth open in astonishment and shock.

'I beg your pardon? You would take over the practice?'

'My mother obviously wanted me to—and,

anyway, what would be the point of having the house without a job up here?'

'And did she have any other wishes I should know about?' asked Christa tartly. 'You say she mentioned other things in this letter?'

Lachlan Maguire hesitated then said crisply, 'Nothing of consequence.'

Christa took a deep breath and swallowed hard, trying to compose herself. 'I suppose it had never occurred to me that I wouldn't become the senior partner after Isobel retired—we'd never really discussed it. Perhaps having worked here six years I assumed I'd earned that right…'

Lachlan looked thoughtfully at Christa. 'It must be a shock, but having started the practice and built it up, perhaps she had the right to say whom she would like to succeed her.'

'Isobel didn't build the practice up on her own—I think other people came into it too,' said Christa sharply, a slight flush of anger on her cheeks. 'I rather take exception to someone just waltzing into the practice without any discussion and…'

Lachlan held his hand up. 'Whoa! Keep your

hair on! I haven't decided to take it all on yet—it's a big decision, leaving my job in Australia.' He flicked a quick glance at her flushed face and said lightly, 'Perhaps we can discuss this over a drink and not in the car park?'

She nodded coolly. 'A good idea—when do you suggest?'

'This evening about six? Come to the house and I'll see what's been left in the drinks cabinet.'

'Come on, then, Titan, we'll be going.' Christa bent down to ruffle the dog's head, and he leaped up and trotted at her heels towards the little terraced house she owned on the village green.

Lachlan watched her slim figure striding away and grimaced. Of all the people his mother had had to choose to be her colleague, he could hardly believe that it should be Angus Lennox's niece! It was extraordinary that Isobel should have picked Christa, of all people, to work with her. And now there was this poignant letter, Isobel's dying request…

Lachlan felt his throat constrict as he reread it in his mind's eye, urging him to take over the practice. That was a reasonable enough wish and one that left him with a mixture of emotions—a poignant regret that they hadn't talked about it before her death, and pride and relief that Isobel must still have loved him enough to want him to carry on her work.

It was her other bizarre suggestion that had floored him—it was ridiculous, almost cheeky! Perhaps it was even a joke—but for some reason he was pretty sure his mother had meant every word, he could even hear her voice with that soft hint of determination in it.

He shook his head tiredly. He couldn't think about it now, his brain was a jumble of contrasting thoughts. Lachlan turned abruptly back towards the house and went in, slamming the door irritably behind him.

'How could she do this to me—never warning me that Lachlan was her preferred choice for senior partner?' muttered Christa angrily, as she opened her front door and went into the kitchen to make a cup of restorative tea.

A torrent of aggrieved feelings had been building up inside her as she'd walked home, a bitter sense of injustice mixed with bewilderment that a good friend like Isobel should apparently want a son she hadn't seen for years to take over the practice. Isobel had always said how she hoped that Christa would remain there when she retired, and from that Christa had assumed that she would take the surgery over. How wrong she'd been, she thought sadly.

Christa gazed out of the window at the people crossing the green towards the church, a peaceful scene in the mellow late afternoon light, and gradually she began to calm down. She didn't want to allow this to colour her view of Isobel, who had been so incredibly kind to her, not only when her mother had been ill but also when Christa's affair with Colin had disintegrated. Whatever had happened, Isobel had shown Christa that there was life after a broken heart, and had encouraged her to seek new interests, given her more responsibility in the practice. Christa would be forever grateful for that.

And after all, it was natural for Isobel to leave the house to her son despite their distant relationship—she must still have loved him very much and maybe she felt the job went with the house. Even so, Christa wasn't about to hand control of the practice to this Lachlan—she didn't know him, didn't have an idea of his work or how they'd get on with each other. And one question that persisted—why had he never been to see his mother or, to Christa's knowledge, had any contact with her for so many years? It was a very hard thing to understand—Christa couldn't imagine severing contact with a mother, however difficult relations between them might be.

A sudden image of Lachlan's strong face and unusual eyes floated into Christa's head—he had a tough, rather exacting look about him, a look that indicated he wouldn't suffer fools gladly. The kind of man who got what he wanted. She imagined that he could be manipulative—just like many a good-looking man—and probably thought he could talk Christa round to anything with his flattering tongue and celebrity looks.

Well, she was prepared and she'd jolly well show him she wouldn't be pushed around by another man in a hurry! She certainly deserved just as much say in the running of things, having worked for Isobel for six years.

She scribbled down some bullet points that she would put to him—she wouldn't simply step meekly aside.

'I've got to be firm, Titan,' she informed the dog.

Titan looked up from his comfortable basket and thumped his tail sleepily in agreement.

Lachlan Maguire towelled himself down vigorously after his shower in the tepid water, the hottest temperature he could raise from Ardenleigh's antiquated boiler. The whole place needed gutting—a fortune would have to be spent on it. He looked round at the cracked plaster and suspicion of damp on the walls, the stained bath and peeling lino floor. It was basically a handsome house, but where to start?

Years ago, before he'd left home, the house had been beautifully kept—light, bright chintzes in the sitting room, an airy dining room with lovely old furniture and a huge bay window that looked over the garden. Now there was an unkempt and uncared-for feel about the place—it felt sad and neglected.

Lachlan wound the towel round his waist and started to shave, peering into the dim mirror, and his bleak reflection stared back at him. A mixture of regret and sadness washed over him as he thought of the naïve judgemental youth he'd been, blaming his parents totally on the break-up of his family, impulsively moving as far away as he could.

Once he'd loved them dearly—a love that over the years he'd thought had turned to hate. Even now, years later, he could feel the resentment and despair he'd felt as a young lad when his world had seemed to collapse around him.

What an irony it was, therefore, that Isobel had left him the house—and perhaps by way of an apology, or some form of restitution, written that emotional letter, hoping Lachlan would take over her beloved practice. His mother had shown him that she still loved him, and had had faith in him. With a sudden and overwhelming feeling of guilt and sorrow, he realised that it was too late now to tell her that, despite everything, he had still loved her, had still missed her and had often longed to come home and see her again. How stupid he'd been to let his pride get in the way!

Could Lachlan fulfil his mother's last requests? Surely a sense of obligation at least would mean that he should take over the house and the practice. But the other bizarre wish? That might be more difficult to contemplate! Then he grinned wryly as he splashed cold water on his face and patted it dry with one of the cardboard-like towels he'd found in a cupboard. He considered the situation.

Lachlan flicked a hand through his thick, spiky hair to try and tame it and dabbed at a cut on his chin with the towel. He did have some sympathy with Christa—he would probably have felt a good deal of resentment if a strange guy had appeared out of the blue to take over the practice.

She wasn't the kind of girl to accept things meekly, he reflected. He recalled her angry-looking figure at the bottom of the ladder that afternoon, commanding him to come down! He grinned. For some reason he'd rather enjoyed seeing her sherry-coloured eyes snap and sparkle at him when she'd been annoyed.

Christa had no idea of the connection between their two families—and perhaps it was better to keep it that way, although the truth had a habit of coming out when you least expected it.

Then suddenly a wave of exhaustion overcame him. He stretched and yawned. The last few days had been a complete blur. The time from learning that his mother had died to getting a plane from Sydney to London and then eventually arriving in Inverness had seemed endless. When he'd finally arrived in Errin Bridge and seen the solicitor, jet-lag had begun to catch up on him.

Lachlan wandered into one of the bedrooms, stuffed with heavy dark furniture and a huge sagging bedstead. In his exhausted state it looked quite inviting and he flung himself onto it. Just a little kip for a quarter of an hour would do him the world of good. He lay back on the musty pillow and fell into a deep slumber.

Through a fog of sleep Lachlan heard the doorbell ring. He stirred restlessly, trying to ignore it, then heard a dog barking. With a muffled oath he sat up and swung his legs over the side of the bed. The doorbell rang again—whoever it was couldn't wait.

He padded downstairs wearily and opened the front door, realising too late that he was still only dressed in a small towel wrapped round his waist. Christa was standing there, with Titan standing guard by her side.

They stared at each other, his eyes sweeping over her slim figure, elegant in jeans, long black boots and a warm, close-fitting red biker jacket with a black scarf casually looped round her neck. He clapped a hand to his forehead.

'Oh, God! Sorry! I fell asleep after my shower...forgot you were coming.' His austere expression changed to a wry grin. 'I'd have put something on to hide my modesty if I'd known it was you.'

Christa flicked a glance over the lean and athletic body before her. Good God, was ever a man in such superb shape! She wondered crossly why the sight of his bare chest should affect her when it was something she saw routinely in the surgery—but, then, of course, not many of her patients had torsos like Lachlan Maguire!

She tore her glance away and said blandly, 'Don't worry, I've seen it all before… If it's inconvenient, I'll come back another time.'

'No time like the present…' He held the door open and motioned her in. 'If you'll wait in the kitchen I'll put some clothes on—won't be a minute.'

He stepped away as Christa passed him and she caught the faint fresh smell of soap and shaving lotion. She watched as he bounded up the stairs, holding onto the towel, and grimaced to herself when she remembered the way she'd harangued him about being nothing but the scum of the earth! That was the last thing he looked… he had to be the sexiest male on two legs that she'd seen for a very long time. Not, she reminded herself sharply, that she was at all interested in sexy males—they were too sure of themselves, too confident by half and far too duplicitous.

She sat down in the ramshackle kitchen with Titan curled up on an old rug under the window. There were ancient cupboards with broken hinges, an old-fashioned stove on four cast-iron legs and a few dusty shelves with bottles and jam jars jostling for space. Isobel had been a lonely person, living on her own in this big house, and patently had had no interest in cooking if the look of the kitchen was anything to go by. It was almost shocking that she had allowed the house to get into this state—odd, too, when she had been a well-organised and efficient doctor.

If Lachlan was married and came to live in Errin Bridge, how would his wife take to living in a time warp like this? Indeed, would she relish the thought of leaving Australia and coming up to a Scottish backwater?

Engrossed in her thoughts, Christa didn't notice Lachlan at first when he appeared at the door. She was gazing out of the window, her shiny bob of auburn hair framing a profile of a determined little chin and a tip-tilted nose. She was feisty with decided opinions—rather like he was, he acknowledged. He guessed she wasn't about to defer to him in any discussion about the practice.

'I've looked in the drinks cupboard,' he said from the doorway. 'All I can find is whisky and more whisky… Would that be OK?'

Christa jumped with surprise and looked round at him, relieved to see that he was now more modestly attired in jeans and a T-shirt under a corduroy jerkin. 'Yes, please, with a splash of water.'

She watched him as he poured out the drink, his movements neat, unfussy. He handed her a tumbler and she twirled the amber liquid around in her glass, watching the light catch it, and then looked at him warily.

'So. When are you going to decide on whether or not to follow your mother's wishes?'

'I've almost decided, although I do have some matters to discuss with the solicitor,' he admitted. 'If those matters can be resolved and I can find a way to pay for the repairs to the house, then I'm tempted to come back.'

'That's a big decision—to give up your life in Australia,' commented Christa. 'Did you like it there?'

'Certainly I did…' A slight change in expression flickered across his face. 'But I've been there a good while and perhaps it's time to come back to my roots.' He looked across the rolling fields to the side of the house and the sea beyond, lacy with white breakers, and smiled. 'Who wouldn't want to live in the beautiful surroundings of Errin Bridge?'

'And are you married—would your wife mind you moving away from Australia?'

Lachlan laughed. 'No—I've no ties, I'm entirely free… And you? Are you someone's wife or mother?'

Christa took a gulp of the whisky and it trailed fire down her throat. 'Oh, no,' she said airily. 'I'm not into commitment—far too much to do with my life first.'

'How very wise,' he murmured.

Christa changed the subject abruptly—she certainly didn't want to dwell on the past, especially her relationship with Colin Maitland. She drew out her list of bullet points from her bag and looked at Lachlan challengingly.

'Now, can we get down to business? I have to say bluntly I'm not happy that you can just leap into the practice here as senior partner—I can't believe that Isobel wouldn't understand how I'd feel about it all.'

Lachlan put his hands up. 'Hey! Not so fast! You have a habit of jumping to conclusions, don't you? I'm certainly not proposing to leap into anything, but if I'm to have full responsibility for the buildings, I need to have at least an equal say.'

'Fair enough…but, to be blunt, I'd like to know what experience you have. I know nothing about you.'

'Of course!' The austere face broke into a grin. 'I've been with the Flying Doctor service in Australia for a few years, and I'm quite brilliant at small ops…a dab hand at dealing with every imaginable situation, from snake bites and childbirth to extracting teeth and acute dehydration…'

Christa couldn't resist smiling at him, her cheeks dimpling. He certainly had all the Maguire charm of persuasion, and underneath that sometimes dour expression he seemed to have a sense of humour. But there were still questions as to why he'd leave his life in Australia so easily.

'You have an interesting job there—why give it all up, even if your mother has left you Ardenleigh?' she asked curiously.

He swirled the whisky round in his glass, the smile fading from his face. 'Time to move on, I guess. I'd been thinking of leaving for some time—it was a great life, but it wasn't Errin Bridge. I think I always hoped to come back here some day.'

But not while your mother was alive, thought Christa, puzzled as to why that should be. She tapped her fingers on the table thoughtfully. 'We'd have to get on with each other…'

A raised eyebrow. 'You're bound to be able to get on with an easygoing guy like me!'

She looked at Lachlan sardonically. 'You think? Suppose we don't, and incredibly I find you're impossible to work with? I'm certainly not going to be the one leaving the practice.'

'Let's give it six months—if the incredible happens and you find you can't work with me, then I shall go!' He took another swig of his drink. 'I'll give you the e-mail address of my boss near Sydney—I can guarantee he'll give me a good reference.'

Christa nodded coolly. She wasn't about to go overboard and welcome him with open arms yet. 'I imagine it will be very different from the Australian Outback. You ought to know something about the practice here...'

'People still have the same illnesses, I suppose. What about local hospitals?'

'St Luke's, about eight miles away, is the nearest, but we have a small cottage hospital in the town, mostly for post-operative use when patients living in outlying districts have no one to look after them. And we have a minor injuries unit at the surgery.'

'Sounds good. Anything else?'

'You'd have to be good at walking up mountains. We're the back-up team if things go wrong up there—and you'd be amazed how often that happens in the summer with the tourists.'

He raised an impressed eyebrow. 'You're a Jill of all trades, then. I remember going out to help before I went to medical school. I enjoyed it, so you can count me in.'

'You sound as if you've made up your mind!'

'I suppose I have,' he said cautiously. 'A germ of an idea came to me when I was resting upstairs about how I might raise some money to restore Ardenleigh House—and that makes me feel quite excited about the future here.'

'So that's a yes, is it?'

He nodded and smiled. 'Probably. As I said, there are just one or two things I need to clarify, but I think they can be resolved.'

'Then we'll need to hammer out some sort of an agreement for the partnership…' A moment's misgiving as Christa flicked a glance at his self-assertive face—she could imagine he'd want his own way on quite a few matters, and she certainly wouldn't give in easily! 'When can you start? How much notice do you have to give?'

'I'm due a few weeks' holiday—I'll use that in lieu of notice.'

'What about your stuff—won't you have to go back and pack?'

He shrugged. 'I travel light so I've brought

all I need. I've a friend who'll arrange to have things shipped out if I need them.'

Christa bit her lip. Was she being foolish, leaping into work with someone she knew nothing about? Then she gave a mental shrug. The man was here and available and she was desperate for help, and in any case how could she stop him? She'd just have to hope he was efficient.

'I'll see you, then, in a week, with the proviso of a six months' probationary period to see if it works, and that we'll be equal partners. I'll put it in writing.' She looked at her watch and stood up. 'I've got to fly and see my mother. I usually pop in on a Sunday evening.'

'Your mother still lives in the area?'

'Oh, yes. She has a little flat near me and she loves it there. She's made a good life for herself since my father died.'

Christa got up and Lachlan went with her to the door. It was getting dark now and the courtyard light made deep shadows against the walls. Drops of rain had started to fall, and there was a soft, sweet smell of damp earth on the cool air. Autumn was on its way, and soon the soft purple heather and greens of the glens would be replaced by sparkling frost and snow on the hills.

He'd missed those definitive seasons, and although he'd had a ball in Australia, there had been times when a certain tune, the waft of scent of the sea, or a Scottish voice passing him on the street, would stir a longing in him to be back in Errin Bridge. He should have come back before, he thought sadly, and not allowed his stubborn nature to dictate his life.

Titan, standing beside Christa, suddenly stiffened, the hackles on his neck rising. Then he gave a low growl before breaking into a cacophony of barking.

'What is it, old boy? Calm down…'

Titan took no notice and suddenly darted across the yard, still barking at full pitch.

'There's someone there,' said Lachlan in a low voice, putting a restraining hand on Christa's arm. 'I wouldn't be surprised if this turns out to be one of your pesky thieves.'

CHAPTER TWO

THEY STOOD FOR a moment on the doorstep, looking towards the barns, the outside light from the surgery casting a beam across the courtyard and the ladder that Lachlan had been using. It was raining heavily now and the sound of it drummed on the roof and made huge puddles across the yard.

Then above that sound there was a muffled crash as if something heavy had fallen. A scream came from one of the outbuildings, and a hooded youth ran out into the beam of light, the raindrops silver as they landed on his frightened face. He looked wildly around and then darted back into the building. Titan barked excitedly and rushed after him.

Christa drew in a sharp breath. 'I know that boy—it's Carl Burton. He's a patient! What's he doing in the barn?'

'I'm not waiting to find out,' growled Lachlan. 'Is there a torch anywhere?'

He ran quickly across the yard and Christa flew to the surgery, scrabbling round in a drawer to find a torch, and instinct telling her to grab the emergency medical bag she kept locked in a cupboard by her desk. She was back in the barn inside two minutes.

The light in the outbuilding was dim, but in the torch's beam they saw a boy lying on the floor, ominously still, his legs splayed at an awkward angle. His face was so pale that the large gash over his forehead looked as if it had been painted on. A piece of wood had fallen from the roof and was wedged above him at an angle. Carl Burton crouched by the victim's side and he looked up at Christa and Lachlan with a mixture of fear and bravado on his face.

'Bloody hell,' muttered Lachlan, darting forward and pushing Carl out of the way. 'Let me see what the damage is.'

Carl backed away from the victim. 'Is he dead?' he said, his voice cracking. 'Has he been killed?'

Lachlan put his fingers on the boy's neck to feel his carotid artery. He raised his eyes to Christa's questioning look and nodded. 'He's still with us…better get some help, PDQ.'

'It wasn't my fault,' Carl blurted out. 'Greg saw that ladder. I told him not to climb on the roof, but he did. He was being stupid, standing on one foot and waving his arms about. Then he…he…dropped, like a stone…' He stopped, putting his hands over his face.

'That's why he's got to be treated as quickly as possible.' Lachlan's voice was brusque. 'It's lucky we were here.'

Christa pulled her mobile out of her pocket and flicked it open, punching out numbers. She walked over to the doorway as she spoke, glancing back at Lachlan bent over the victim's body. Christa felt an almighty surge of thankfulness that she wasn't alone in having to cope with things.

'Ambulance and the police services, please—Dr Lennox here from the Ardenleigh Practice in Errin Bridge. I need the air ambulance for a serious leg, head and possible spinal injury to a youth who's fallen from a roof just by the practice. My colleague and I will try and stabilise him, but he needs hospitalisation without delay. If you could inform St Luke's to have an orthopaedic surgeon and anaesthetist on standby, please.'

'We'll have to do our best until they get here,' observed Lachlan. He pulled back the upper lids of the boy's eyes. 'Pupils dilated,' he murmured to himself, then examined the victim's body, checking his head and other visible injuries. 'He's not bleeding too much from this head wound…'

'That's good, isn't it?' Carl looked up at Lachlan hopefully.

'I'm afraid it's not the same as just banging your head on a cupboard. Hitting your head at speed can give rise to arterial bleeding, and he's had a tremendous crack to his forehead, besides his possible back and neck injuries and a broken leg.'

Christa bit her lip. Had the boy's spine survived the impact of falling from the roof? Could they keep him alive until the paramedics arrived with their specialist equipment? She looked closely at the young boy's face, where a bruise was developing around the gash on his forehead.

She drew in her breath. 'Oh, God, I know this guy too…he's Gregory Marsh, aged about sixteen.' Her eyes met Lachlan's. 'Are you thinking acute subdural haematoma?'

He nodded and bent low over the boy, saying clearly, 'Do you know where you are, Gregory?'

After a few seconds the boy whispered, 'I'm in the barn, aren't I?'

'That's right, Gregory, well done. Now, where does it hurt? Can you tell us?'

The boy's eyes fluttered open, his breath rasping, his face contorted with pain. 'My leg… bloody hell, it's my leg,' he muttered.

'You can feel your leg, then?' A measure of relief in Christa's voice.

'Of course I can feel my effing leg…' he croaked. 'It's agony…'

'Let's look at this leg,' said Lachlan briskly. 'Can you cut his jeans?'

Christa used a pair of scissors from the bag to cut the leg of the jeans very gently from the distorted leg. They both looked down at the limb, which was gashed and swollen. Protruding through the gash was a white piece of bone.

Christa grimaced. 'A compound fracture, not very nice…'

'Poor blighter—it needs splinting.'

'That's OK. We've got some we use for the mountain rescue work. I'll get them.'

'Give me your bag of tricks and I'll put some sterile dressings on these open wounds, and give him a ten-mil shot of morphine for the pain.' Lachlan looked down reassuringly at Gregory and laid a comforting hand on the boy's shoulder. It was a gesture not lost on Christa. Physical touch was an incredibly important and soothing thing, and reassurance could reduce the severity of shock—it was as important a medical tool as any conventional treatment.

'Don't worry, Gregory, you're in good hands and we'll soon have you in hospital.'

Christa went to get the collapsible splints and returned swiftly, snapping the splint joints into place and laying them out. The two doctors worked as gently as possible to immobilise the leg by strapping the limb to the splint, but Lachlan kept flicking a wary look at the beam above them, jammed across most of Gregory's body. Christa heard him suck in his breath.

'Bloody hell—can you hear that beam creaking?' he muttered. 'The whole damn thing could fall on top of us. It has to be moved.'

'I don't know how…' began Christa.

He turned to Carl, watching them mutely, his face as white as a ghost's. 'I tell you what, Carl—you can help me try and push it out of the way.'

'Don't even think of doing that!' Christa's voice was sharp. 'The helicopter will be here soon—'

'And that could be too late. If I could get underneath it, I could lift it out of that gap in the wall and with Carl's support we could push it to one side.'

She stared crossly at Lachlan. 'Suppose you get crushed?'

'If we wait for that damned air ambulance to

come, the boy will need more than a spinal brace and a leg splint.'

Christa got up from Greg's side and pulled at Lachlan's arm. 'Do you want there to be two casualties, for heaven's sake?'

He shook her arm away irritably. 'I'll be OK. We haven't got a choice—look, it's swaying again…'

For a second they looked at each other stubbornly then Christa shrugged, acknowledging that Lachlan was right. They couldn't just ignore the situation—something had to be attempted. She looked around the barn desperately. There were some old packing cases and dust sheets by the wall near Carl. She began dragging them across to Gregory and shouted to Carl.

'Come on! Help me get these over Gregory to protect him before you start tampering with the damn beam—put the sheets over him and then the packing cases like a cage. It might just take the shock if the beam falls.'

'Why can't we just pull him away from it?' asked Carl.

'Because,' said Christa in a low voice, 'we don't

know what damage Gregory's done to his spine. If he's damaged it in the fall, we could sever it.'

They worked feverishly to construct some sort of barrier between Gregory and the chunk of wood wedged over him, then Lachlan slid his body underneath it to the side of the injured boy, so that he could try and shift the beam from where it was so precariously perched. There was a tense silence: Gregory's eyes fluttered open again and he focussed them on Christa.

'What's happening?' he whispered.

Christa's voice was calm. 'Nothing to worry about, Gregory, just making sure the beam's secure. Everything's under control.'

She hoped devoutly that that was the case, and indeed something told her that if anyone could handle an emergency like this, Lachlan Maguire could. She watched him tensely as he manoeuvred the beam, calm but concentrated, no sign of panic. Perhaps she shouldn't have been surprised by his competence—someone who worked with the Flying Doctor service had to be able to think on his feet, quite an asset for someone she was going to work with.

Lachlan pulled the rag from his pocket and wound it round his hand to try and get more purchase. 'Come on, Carl—I know you're in shock, but you've got to help me, for your mate's sake.' His voice was tough, uncompromising. 'Give me a hand to try and shift this. While I push it up, get your arms round it to pull.'

Both men grunted with the effort of trying to shift the wood away from over Gregory's body, and eventually, with a final push and a shout of warning from Lachlan, it fell harmlessly to one side.

'Thank God,' whispered Christa, blowing out her cheeks and closing her eyes in relief. Lachlan climbed stiffly to his feet with a relieved grin and dusted his hands together.

'There you are—nothing to it!' He went across to Carl. 'Thank you for helping there,' he said quietly. 'I couldn't have done it without you. Now, tell me how all this started.'

Carl hung his head and muttered, 'We…we were trying to get at the guttering—we saw the ladder and Greg thought it would be easy. I told him not to, but he started pretending he was a high-wire act and just fell from the beam up there.'

'Were you trying to nick the lead?'

'We didn't think nobody would miss it. We didn't mean any harm, we just needed a bit of cash…' The boy started to shake at the memory of the accident, wrapping his arms round his thin body, rocking slightly on his heels.

Lachlan looked at Carl's white face. 'You feel all right?'

The boy shook his head helplessly as if unable to express just how he felt. 'I…I just can't believe it… Seeing it happen…'

His voice petered out, not equal to describing what he'd just seen, and Lachlan nodded, recognising all the signs of violent emotional shock in the boy. What Carl had witnessed had happened with appalling swiftness, with no time for him to prepare or adjust to the situation. His senses were stunned by the events and Lachlan recognised all the signs of 'onlooker reaction'. He put his arm round Carl's shoulder and drew him to the wall.

'I want you to sit down here. Your body's got

a touch of shock, just as much as if you'd had a physical injury. After a nice hot cup of sweet tea you'll feel much better.'

The boy's face relaxed slightly. He hadn't been expecting any kind words, but they helped to calm him, bring back something of normality to his fractured emotional state. There'd be plenty of condemnation later, thought Lachlan wryly.

Christa attached an oximeter peg to Gregory's finger to get a readout of his vital signs.

'What's it like?' said Lachlan.

Christa grimaced and murmured, 'BP's low, eighty over fifty. Not surprising, and his pulse is thready. How's the pain, Greg?'

The boy stirred slightly but didn't speak, and Lachlan looked at his watch.

'How long are they going to be?' he growled.

Then through the beating of the rain on the roof there was the sudden clatter of a helicopter's rotors overhead, the sound increasing in volume as it descended somewhere near the surgery. Christa sent up a silent prayer—they'd arrived just in the nick of time.

'Where will they land?' asked Lachlan, as he and Christa exchanged relieved glances.

'There's a field beyond the woods at the end of the garden, they'll put down there. It'll only take them a few minutes to get here now.'

Lachlan got to his feet and went to the door to meet them, and very soon three men in bright orange outfits and luminous jerkins with 'Doctor' and 'Paramedic' labels across them came running across the courtyard. Lachlan gave a quick résumé of Gregory's visible injuries and what he and Christa had done so far to stabilise him.

'He'll get a full body scan, and the theatre's on standby,' said the doctor accompanying them. 'He was damn lucky that he had you two near him when he decided to do his sky-walking exploits.'

The paramedics set up a drip and strapped a spinal board on Gregory, with an oxygen mask over his face, and Carl started to sidle surreptitiously towards the door. One of the paramedics stopped him, looking at his pale face and trembling hands.

'Have you hurt yourself?' he enquired.

'No. I'm OK.' The voice was sullen, uncooperative.

'Why don't you come with us for a check-up, eh?'

A vehement shake of the head. 'I'm OK, I tell you. I'm going home.' He jerked his head in Gregory's direction. 'He'll be OK now, won't he? You don't need me.'

'Oh, yes, we do, my friend.' A burly policeman had appeared at the barn door and stood in front of the boy. 'We need a few names and addresses, young man. A little bit of information as to how this happened, if you please.'

He led Carl out of the building. The boy looked pathetic, shoulders drooping, and his jeans hung so low around his hips they were barely able to stay up. He looked back at Lachlan and muttered, 'Will Greg be all right?'

'Hopefully, but he won't be climbing around on roofs for a while,' remarked Lachlan drily.

The emergency services had gone and it had stopped raining as Christa and Lachlan walked back across the yard, Titan trotting proudly beside them, as if aware that he had been the first to alert them to the emergency. Lachlan stretched, flexing his stiff lower back, which had taken the strain of him pushing the beam away, and took a deep breath of the clear air. The velvety night sky had cleared of cloud and was twinkling with a tapestry of stars. In the distance was the sound of the sea, whooshing in and out on the beach.

'God, that smells good. How I've missed that special Highland tang,' he murmured. 'I'd forgotten just how intoxicating the air can be in this little corner of the world.'

'How many years since you've been here, then?'

A short silence, then he said roughly, 'Too many…but it's good to be back.'

Christa looked at the bleak expression on his face, and felt a moment's impatience. If he had missed home so much, why hadn't he come back occasionally to see his mother, a woman on her own? Christa was tempted to ask outright what had kept him away, but she sensed that that would be a question too far at the moment.

She pushed that thought to the back of her mind. So much had happened in the last hour and she should have felt drained, but instead she felt the kick of adrenalin after a job well done. Together they'd managed to keep Gregory alive, to retrieve a situation that had looked almost impossible.

She was profoundly grateful that Lachlan Maguire had been there—almost unwillingly she admitted that he'd been pretty impressive, efficient and reliable. Just the kind of person one would want in an emergency. She flicked a glance at his tall figure beside her—perhaps, after all, she was prepared to believe that he was as good as he said he was at his job!

'I…I'm glad you were here. In fact, if you hadn't been, I think the ending could have been very different. Thank you,' she said.

'Do you think our young friends are the culprits who've been nicking stuff from here?' he said.

'Could be… They're both patients but I haven't seen them for ages. From his odd behaviour on the roof I wonder if Gregory's on something

Anyway, they'll do plenty of tests at St Luke's.' Christa sighed. 'I'll bet his parents don't know what he's up to—or are turning a blind eye to the situation.'

'They're going to find out soon,' said Lachlan grimly.

'God—it was a bit scary, like being back in A and E again. I thought we'd lost him, and he had so many injuries…' Then she puffed out her cheeks, laughing up at Lachlan, her amber eyes dancing with relief. 'But it was a great feeling that we kept him going till the paramedics came, wasn't it?'

He looked down at Christa's dust-covered face turned up to his, and a feeling of affinity with a colleague after a job well done intensified into something else—the treacherous flare of sexual attraction. For a second his eyes roamed over her heart-shaped face and wide eyes, as if seeing her properly for the first time, and he sucked in his breath. Good God, she was absolutely ravishing…and desirable.

Almost absent-mindedly he touched her cheek, wiping away some mud and allowing his finger to trail down her jaw. He smiled at her, then without warning he bent his head down and brushed her lips with his, slowly, deliberately, fiercely.

'You shouldn't look so bloody beautiful,' he whispered against her ear.

Christa remained motionless for a second then touched her lips where his had been. They felt full, tingling and soft, and for a second she was bewildered. Where the hell had that come from, or had she just imagined it?

Then a feeling of outrage swept through her—Lachlan Maguire had the cheek of the devil!

'What the hell do you think you're doing?' she demanded icily.

He laughed. 'Come on—you've got your head-mistress look on your face again! It was just an expression of thanks for a job well done. Am I to sit on the naughty step?'

'Don't be ridiculous.'

'We seemed to work rather well together, that's all! A spur-of-the-moment thing!'

'You took a damn liberty!'

He looked rather penitent, but his blue eyes

danced at her mischievously, and he gave his most disarming grin. 'It was just a little gesture of, er, thanks,' he protested. 'I didn't mean to offend you—it was a sort of compliment!'

Christa opened her mouth to say something cutting then shut it again because for a minute Lachlan looked so like a naughty schoolboy that, despite herself, she felt an urge to giggle. Obviously the impulsive kiss that had sent her reeling meant absolutely nothing to him—just a bit of fun.

And yet, she admitted to herself, the truth was that every single nerve in *her* body had seemed to respond with a longing for something more, something much more intimate, something that would repeat the fireworks that had seemed to explode so suddenly around her as his mouth had plundered hers. It was as if a switch had been thrown, and something that hadn't worked for a long time had been kicked into action.

She pushed these thoughts to the back of her mind and decided the best response was to try and treat the episode with dignified aversion.

She buttoned up her jacket, and said rather

pompously, 'Don't expect a repeat performance, Lachlan—I took you on as a work colleague, not a rake!'

He burst into laughter. 'Come on…it doesn't suit you to take life so seriously, Dr Lennox! I thought you secretly wanted to press your lovely body close to mine…'

This was a little too near the truth. Christa flushed and said indignantly, 'Don't be silly!'

Lachlan assumed a more contrite expression. 'Don't be cross. I'm sorry if I took you by surprise, but I know we'll make a very good partnership.'

Those amazing eyes danced winningly into Christa's, almost like a caress in itself, and although she was really mad at him, she couldn't help smiling back. They were going to have to work together amicably, she told herself, so there was no point in maintaining a frigid atmosphere. She'd just have to be on her guard in the future. After all, wasn't it typical of some males to take relationships as casually as picking sweets from a jar?

Then, dangerously, the thought echoed in her

mind that if one kiss could practically send her into orbit, making her heart clatter in her chest and a thousand butterflies seem as if they were fluttering somewhere around in her stomach, what would it be like if they made real, proper love?

Titan whimpered and Christa bent down to ruffle the little dog's head, grateful of the distraction to her thoughts. 'Poor old Titan, you want your supper. In all the fuss I'd forgotten that. Come on, then—home time now.' She turned to Lachlan and said lightly, 'See you soon.'

As she walked home through the still night Christa's heart beat a tattoo against her ribs, and even her legs felt slightly wobbly. It had been so long since any man had caressed her or kissed her—so long since she'd fancied anyone enough to do so. But out of the blue, out of nowhere, had come a man she didn't know at all, sending her into a spin! She came to her front door and her hand trembled slightly as she tried to put the key in the lock.

'What's the matter with me, Titan?' she asked the little dog. 'Have I gone completely mad?'

* * *

Lachlan closed the door, leaning against the wall for a minute, and took a deep breath, reflecting on the effect two soft full lips could have on a man when they were pressed to his mouth. He hadn't expected his body to respond so urgently, and wondered what on earth had possessed him to kiss Christa after a mere afternoon's acquaintance. Then he grinned to himself—because she was so damned beautiful, of course, and didn't the thought of shocking that rather prim, head-mistressy personality rather appeal?

He was used to casual relationships—never commit yourself because they never lasted, was his mantra. Take your pleasure where you could. He wasn't going to make the same mistake his parents had—get married, supposedly for life, and then destroy the family with a bitter and cruel break-up.

Perhaps he'd gone a step too far with Christa Lennox, expecting her to take his kiss as casually as he had—but life was for living and having fun, wasn't it? Except, of course, he'd forgotten that one person he should keep at arm's length was someone from the Lennox family. And neither had he bargained for the fierce longing he now had to kiss Christa again—and more.

'Isobel's *son*? I don't believe it!' Alice Smith's large blue eyes looked at Christa in amazement, and she paused in mid-action as she pulled open a filing-cabinet drawer. 'He's a bit late, isn't he? Isobel's funeral was a week ago!'

'Nobody knew where he was, and he only heard she'd died a few days ago,' explained Christa.

Christa and the two receptionists, Alice Smith and Ginny Calder, were having a quick cup of coffee before the Monday morning surgery, and Christa had been regaling them with the previous day's events in the barn. Both girls goggled in disbelief at Christa.

'Where's he been, then, all these years?' asked Ginny, the elder of the two receptionists, her eyes popping with surprise behind her thick-lensed glasses.

'He's been working in Australia—it took a time to find out where he was.'

Alice stuffed some papers into the files and said thoughtfully, 'It was sad, wasn't it—to stay away as long as he did. I wonder what happened.'

'I remember him,' recalled Ginny. 'He was a handsome lad, and I know he was the apple of his mother's eye. She was so proud of him.'

'Well, what went wrong?' asked Alice bluntly. 'How come she never spoke about him?'

Ginny shook her head. 'No one knows, except that Isobel's husband left her around the time that Lachlan went off to college—and, of course, Lachlan was never seen again. How long's he staying?'

Christa put her cup of coffee down on the desk. 'Actually, it's not just a flying visit—he's going to work here permanently. Isobel left him a letter saying that she wanted him to take over the practice. And he's decided to do that. She's left the house to him.'

'What?' Alice closed the filing-cabinet drawer with a crash and turned to her in amazement. 'But...but I thought you would be taking over... It doesn't seem fair.'

'It's OK, Alice. We've talked it over, and he's

coming in as an equal partner. He understands that, at least for a trial of six months. And anyway we need another doctor, that's for sure. Even before Isobel died we were pretty stretched.'

'Since Colin Maitland left, I suppose… I hope Lachlan's nothing like *him*,' said Ginny sharply, then watching Christa's face she grimaced and clapped her hand over her mouth. 'Oh, I'm sorry, love, I shouldn't have brought up the subject. But you're over Colin now, aren't you?'

Christa smiled brightly. 'Of course I'm over him,' she said robustly. 'I can assure you I won't be taken in by any other con men, however charming!'

'And *is* he charming, this mysterious Lachlan?'

Christa shrugged, trying to look as casual as possible. 'He wasn't so charming when I thought he was a burglar—he was up on the roof inspecting the gutter, and I shouted at him. I got a frosty reception, I can tell you!'

'We want more information than that!' protested Alice. 'Is he single or married, good looking?'

'Now, why do you want to know that?' teased

Christa. 'You've got a lovely boyfriend. But for general information, yes, he says he's single, and I suppose some people would say he's not bad looking. Not that I find him attractive,' she lied.

Of course the truth was that she'd found it difficult to get that mind-blowing kiss from the night before out of her head. To him it had been just a casual brush of flesh on flesh, but in her imagination she could still feel the imprint of that sensual mouth on hers, and the feeling of exploding stars and fireworks it had produced! She took a deep slurp of coffee, hoping the girls wouldn't notice the blush she was sure was spreading over her cheeks.

'Ah!' Alice said with satisfaction, her eyes meeting Ginny's with meaning.

'What do you mean, "Ah"?' Christa looked sternly at Alice and Ginny. 'I can assure you both I'm off men for good, however eligible. I can promise you that if George Clooney were to go down on bended knee and give me a million pounds to marry him, I'd send him off with a flea in his ear! I've no ambition to have a wedding ring on my finger!'

A discreet cough from the doorway and they all whirled round. Lachlan was standing there, a suspicion of laughter in his startling blue eyes, but the expression on his face was impassive.

Christa's cheeks crimsoned, and she jumped up in a flustered way, swallowing whole the biscuit she was eating. Had the darned man heard her inane comment about marriage as he'd stood there?

'Sorry to interrupt you all,' he said smoothly. 'I know I'm not starting work until next week, but I just wanted to know if you'd had any word about how that young boy is from last night's accident…'

Christa rearranged her features quickly from shock to welcome. 'Oh, Lachlan, it's you!' She turned to Alice and Ginny and cleared her throat. 'This is Lachlan Maguire—Isobel's son. Alice and Ginny are the backbone of the practice, Lachlan. We couldn't work without them.'

He looked like someone out of central casting for the lead in a medical drama, she thought, noting irritably how Alice goggled at him with frank admiration. He unleashed a charming smile.

'Then I must keep on the right side of them!'

'I was telling them what happened yesterday,' she explained, then felt her heart begin to race as she remembered just what *had* happened between them after attending the accident.

Lachlan grinned, his eyes holding hers rather too long. 'Plenty happened, that's for sure! I was pushed in at the deep end all right.'

Christa looked away hastily and added some more sugar to her coffee, stirring it vigorously. Alice looked at Lachlan rather like a puppy given a special treat.

'I believe you're going to be working here with us permanently,' she enthused.

'Yes, that's right. I know it'll be a steep learning curve, but I'll do my best. I look forward to getting to know you all.'

He smiled urbanely at them, and Christa could see Alice melting under his easy charm, although Ginny looked more wary. Perhaps, thought Christa, she was a little more cynical than Alice, wondering just why a son should lose touch with a lovely woman like Isobel, then suddenly appear out of the blue after she'd died.

'A cup of coffee?' enquired Alice, still staring at him as if mesmerised.

'Thank you, just a quick one. I guess you're pretty busy and I don't want to hold you up. As I say, I just wanted to find out about the young lad who was injured last night.'

Christa nodded. 'I rang the hospital a few minutes ago. He's injured vertebrae in his back, and he's being operated on this morning for his leg—he'll pull through, though.'

'That's the good news I was hoping to hear before I see the builders this morning. There is one more thing, however. I wondered if it would help if I started on a part-time basis this week—I could get to know the ropes, and if I came with you on one or two visits it would familiarise me with the area again, after so long away.'

Of course it would help. Christa had been sleepless for many nights, wondering how she could cope with the work that was piling up. But she wasn't so sure that being close to Lachlan Maguire was a good thing so soon after her experience with him the night before. She'd rather have liked that episode to fade into the past.

'Oh, I don't think there's any need to—'

'I think that's a great idea,' interrupted Ginny. 'You've been working yourself to a frazzle over the past weeks, Christa. You accept any help that's offered!' She turned to Lachlan. 'Visits are usually done around midday to two o'clock after morning surgery.'

Dear Ginny—she was like a mother hen where she, Christa, was concerned, and she'd been marvellous when Isobel had died, staying late to reorganise surgeries, bringing Christa meals to eat at the surgery. But sometimes she was just a little too fussy!

'Right!' Lachlan said briskly. 'I'll be back, then. See you later.'

When he'd gone, Alice turned to Christa and said accusingly, 'You misled us there! You said he wasn't bad looking…'

'Well?' asked Christa innocently.

'You ought to go for an eye test…he's absolutely *gorgeous*!'

'Beauty,' said Christa grimly, as she picked

up a pile of blood results and went towards the door, 'is in the eye of the beholder!'

'Quite so,' agreed Ginny tersely, as she reached out to answer the phone.

'Will you listen to yourselves?' demanded Alice in disbelief. 'I can tell you, that man's made my pulse go into overdrive! You two must be made of stone!'

Lachlan stood for a moment before he got into the car and looked back towards the surgery, amusement flickering across his face. So Christa Lennox wouldn't get married for a million pounds—even to George Clooney! What the hell had brought that on, a bad experience perhaps?

He grinned to himself. It was a delicious irony that she should say that she wouldn't marry at any price, when one of his mother's ridiculous suggestions in her letter to him had been that he should get married. And that, of all people, Christa Lennox should be the bride!

Well, that was one proposition that wouldn't be fulfilled! He was damned if he'd be manipulated by his mother from beyond the grave, however much he regretted her death and wanted to atone for his quarrel with her.

CHAPTER THREE

'COME ON, TITAN! In you get!'

Titan sprang into the boot of the car and stood up with his front paws on the back seat, looking around eagerly.

'He seems to enjoy going out on visits,' remarked Lachlan as he folded himself up to fit in Christa's little car.

'Oh, he's spoilt rotten—all my regulars seem to love him, especially at our first port of call. Fred was a shepherd and misses his sheepdog dreadfully. She died only a few months ago, so he loves to spoil Titan.'

Christa started the car and it did its usual little jumps and jerks to get going. She felt self-conscious and tense boxed up in this small space with Lachlan, extremely aware of how close he was to her, exuding sex appeal. The faint smell of shaving lotion and the warm tweedy smell of his jacket drifted over to her.

'Have you had this car serviced recently?' asked Lachlan, rubbing his knee as it hit the dashboard sharply and brushing his hand against Christa's as she changed gear. She inhaled quickly as something like a little electric shock of excitement flickered through her at the unexpected touch.

'Er, what?' she said, flustered. 'Oh, no, it hasn't been serviced for a while—I keep meaning to make an appointment. It's something to do with the clutch, I think—sorry about that.'

She glanced at Lachlan's long legs doubled up in the cramped space of the passenger seat. Her car certainly wasn't designed for a hunky guy of over six feet! In fact, the space in the car seemed to have diminished since he'd got in. She'd slept fitfully the previous night, her mind racing over the dramatic events that had taken place, but the thing that stayed with her in 3D clarity, and much to her irritation, was her reaction to Lachlan's kiss. Like the rerunning of a recording, she went over and over it in her mind, reliving the total surprise of it all and the heavenly sensation of his firm mouth on hers, the odd feeling of something interrupted when she'd pulled away from him.

She turned on the car radio to distract herself, irritated that her mind seemed to be fixated on the man, then turned it off again when all she got was loud static and a humming sound.

'You won't get good reception in these hills,' commented Lachlan. 'We'll just be forced to talk to each other, I'm afraid!'

Christa was aware that he had turned to look at her, a quirky smile on his lips. Perhaps, she thought with embarrassment, he could read her mind! She gripped the steering-wheel tightly and started to talk quickly.

'You said you'd had an idea to raise money to do up Ardenleigh. What was it?'

'It was just a vague idea—I've not thought it through properly, but it's to do with the fact that the place has so much land. It might be a good idea to make more use of it…'

'What do you mean?'

'I don't know if it will be feasible, but there's a

hell of a lot of land attached to the house—land that takes in several fields down to the river, which I can't possibly look after. I wondered about developing it as a holiday complex and leisure centre. Perhaps a nine-hole golf course.'

'*What?*' Christa's head whipped round to gaze at him in horror, and the car swerved alarmingly.

'Hey…steady! You're driving a car, remember?' Lachlan looked at the sudden angry flush of her cheeks and raised his eyebrow. 'You don't sound very pleased. What's wrong with the idea?'

She knew she was being unreasonable. After all, Lachlan had only put the suggestion forward tentatively. But the very idea of him thinking of such a thing when he hadn't lived in the area for years, had only just arrived, was ridiculous. It would spoil the whole atmosphere of the pretty little village, and at the moment there was a beautiful walk over the hills that started through that very wood. Perhaps if he'd helped his mother more over the past years, Christa thought angrily, the house might not have deteriorated, and there'd be no need to spend so much money on it.

'What's right with the idea, you mean! I think it's totally mad—you can't just appear after years away and put a ghastly complex in the middle of this idyllic countryside. Hundreds of cars, concreting over beautiful fields…it…it's ridiculous!'

He laughed. 'I don't intend to concrete over the beautiful fields. There'll be some well-designed chalets in the woods, perhaps a really good gym and a small golf course. It'll bring some much-needed employment to the area.'

'But at what cost to the countryside?' protested Christa. 'It'll change the whole character of the place. Besides which, I have a friend who runs a small gym in the village—it'll ruin Richie's business.'

He leaned back in his seat and shrugged. 'It's just a bit of healthy competition. I've got to raise money to do up the house somehow. It could solve a lot of financial difficulties, and give something more to the area that would help young lads like our friends Carl and Greg.' He looked at her sardonically. 'Perhaps you need to think about it.'

'I don't need to think about it. I know it stinks.'

His face hardened and he said drily, 'Fortunately, it's not your decision to make, and you can always object if and when the plans are put forward, but I'm pretty sure it has a lot to recommend it. And one thing I do know—although my mother and I had our differences, it was obviously her wish I have the house. I intend to abide by her wishes.'

All except one, he thought wryly—her wish that he should marry Christa was a step too far!

Christa flicked a cold glance at him. She guessed he was a man who got what he wanted—charming when he wanted to be but nevertheless a dominating character who could ultimately control a situation and steer things his way. There was an inner steel she detected about Lachlan Maguire, which probably brooked no opposition. On the other hand, she thought with spirit, she wasn't about to let him walk roughshod with his schemes without pointing out some of the disadvantages.

An icy silence descended between them, and both of them stared straight ahead. In two minutes the atmosphere seemed to have plummeted! Christa gritted her teeth, wondering how on earth two people with diverse opinions like they seemed to have could possibly work together.

She glanced at Lachlan's implacable profile and cursed her impulsiveness at agreeing in such a precipitate way to work with this man. Then she shrugged inwardly—the deed was done and they had to work together now. Of course she should have thought before opening her mouth. It was stupid to start off on the wrong note, and after all, she conceded, this development scheme was only an idea of Lachlan's at the moment.

They had come to a viewpoint on the road that showed the valley below with the inlet from the sea snaking into it and the majestic hills and mountains stretching far out into the distance. Christa skidded to a halt in the layby, the car facing the view. 'I'm sorry,' she said quietly. 'I should never have flown off the handle like that. But do look! How could you think of defiling countryside like that?'

Lachlan's expression softened and he smiled at her. 'Apology accepted,' he murmured.

He leaned forward and scanned the scenery. It was one of those nippy autumn days with a foretaste of winter, the sky a piercing blue and the trees turning into a magical kaleidoscope of reds, oranges and scarlet, interspersed with green.

'It all looks just the same, I'm glad to say,' he said softly. 'I can remember it all—that special magic and colour that the Highlands possess. Soon those hills will have a white cap of snow on them, and all the trees will have lost their leaves.' He turned to look at her. 'I promise you, Christa, I would never think of defiling the place.'

Christa raised her eyebrows cynically. Sincerity seemed to blaze out of his eyes. But she'd heard men make promises before when in the end they'd wanted their own way.

'I'll hold you to that,' she growled.

'Trust me, please. Now I'm back I realise how much of my heart is here, how many of my earliest memories remain with me. Why, I recall fishing in the loch somewhere along this road when I was a kid. I don't want to change the place.'

He smiled beguilingly at her and Christa's irritation with his ideas began to fade, despite her misgivings.

'You'll be thinking of Loch Fean,' she said. 'It's up in the hills fairly near to where we're going.'

'My friend Colin and I used to go off for the day together when we were kids.' Lachlan turned to look at her. 'Didn't Colin work in the practice for a time?'

Christa's foot hit the accelerator rather hard as she set off again, and they skidded round a bend on two wheels. Lachlan grabbed the dashboard as they missed the other side of the road by inches, and she wrenched the steering-wheel back, wondering what on earth he thought of her driving.

'Sorry! Sorry! Foot slipped! Yes…' she said lightly. 'Colin worked for a while in the practice, but he left and works in a practice a few miles away.'

'I haven't spoken to him for years—I wonder what happened to him?'

'Oh, he got married…' Her voice was offhand.

'So old Colin got married—I never thought he was the type to make it to the altar! Was he at my mother's funeral?'

'Yes, he was there with his wife.' The familiar pang, mixed with sadness, fluttered through her when she recalled Colin standing with his beautiful pregnant wife at the funeral.

The car shuddered to a halt as she stopped at a cross-roads, turning right towards her patient's home. She changed the subject from Colin and his wife to the patient they were going to visit.

'By the way, we're going to see Fred Logan—he's eighty-seven and lives with Bessie, his wife. She and Fred enjoy verbal scraps with each other, but both of them are very frail.'

Lachlan smiled. 'Ah, so Fred Logan's the shepherd you were talking about? He used to give us chocolate mints if he saw us fishing. He and his wife were very kind to us. I'd like to see him again. Is it just a regular check-up, then?'

'Lorna Storey, the community nurse, told me

this morning that she didn't like the look of him when she checked him at the weekend after a fall he had. Like a lot of the independent souls around here, he refuses to believe or admit he's ill.'

'Is it his heart?'

'Partly—he has congestive cardiac failure for which he's on vasodilator drugs, but his immediate problem is his cut hand and she's worried it may become infected. I've brought some antibiotics with me to save Lorna coming out again. He hardly ever gets down to the village.'

'Does he have a family?'

'A son, Ian, who works in Inverness. He does his best, but his own wife works at weekends and they have two children, so it's difficult for him to get away. He'd like his parents to go and live nearer them, but being an independent couple they're resisting that. Lorna wants me to persuade them to have some daily help.'

She turned into a long, bumpy drive, with stone walls on either side and multiple potholes on the surface. At the end could be seen a small cottage with smoke curling straight up into the air from one of the chimneys.

'Here we are! By the way, take a few lungfuls of fresh air before you go in—Fred likes his pipe!'

Christa knocked on the door and then opened it, and Titan trotted in. It was cold in the room, although Fred was sitting by a peat fire, wrapped in an old shawl. He was wreathed in smoke from the pipe he was puffing, and Titan bounded up to him, putting his nose on the old man's knee.

'Ah, Titan, you wee thing—it's good to see you. Bessie! Bessie! It's the doctor—bring some treats for the dog now!'

A tiny little woman with the hunched back of someone afflicted by curvature of the spine came out of a back room, drying her hands on a towel and smiling a welcome.

'Ah—there you are, Doctor! It's good to see you, and little Titan. We've got his special dog biscuits in case he came.'

'No wonder he loves coming here,' remarked Christa as she watched Titan skid across the floor to Fred's wife and sit watching her patiently until she produced the longed-for treat. 'But I've not come so that Titan can be spoiled by you! I hear from Lorna that Fred's had a fall and cut his hand badly.'

'Aye, and he's in a bad mood today, won't have any breakfast. I tell you he'd rather have that filthy pipe than food! I've told him there's nearly fifty years of pollution in this house! Perhaps he'll take notice of you and stop smoking.'

'I doubt he will, Bessie, I've told him often enough. Anyway…' Christa drew Lachlan forward '…I've brought someone with me you may recognise—he says Fred used to give him chocolate mints many years ago when he was fishing in the loch. Lachlan Maguire!'

'Well, I'm damned,' quavered Fred. 'Can you believe it, Bessie? It's Isobel's son! We haven't seen you for many a year. I remember you when you were just a wee lad, fishing with your friend…'

Bessie beamed at him. 'You used to go past the cottage with your bikes!'

'And you used to come out with some shortbread—we loved that.' Lachlan smiled.

The old lady put her hand on Lachlan's sleeve and said gently, 'We were so sorry about your mother's passing, my dear, she was a very good woman. And I know she was so proud of you.'

'I think everyone around here was very fond of her,' said Lachlan. He looked down at the carpet, bunching his fists in his pockets, and Christa wondered how difficult it was for him to meet the local people who remembered him and his mother in happier times.

Fred looked at him over his glasses. 'And where did you get to all these years?'

'In Australia with the Flying Doctor service.'

Bessie looked impressed. 'My goodness—so far away! And have you got a family of your own now?'

'I'm afraid not, Bessie—I don't think I'm the marrying kind!'

'Nonsense!' said Bessie firmly. 'There'll be someone in this world just waiting to meet you, somewhere! You young people probably think it will never happen, but it will!'

'That's nice to know, isn't it?' He grinned. 'Although I have heard it said that some single people around here wouldn't get married for a million pounds!' For a second Lachlan's dancing eyes locked with Christa's.

So he *had* heard what she'd said to Alice and Ginny, thought Christa. A blush of embarrassment flooded her cheeks, and a sudden nervous urge to giggle overcame her, which she disguised by blowing her nose.

Fred drew on his pipe and looked at Lachlan keenly under his bushy eyebrows. 'Bessie and I thought it was cut and dried that you were going to join your mother when you'd qualified, and then you disappeared…' he growled.

'I suppose it was a sad time for the lad—he needed to get away…' interspersed Bessie.

Christa flicked a covert look at Lachlan. She was learning quite a few tantalising things about Lachlan's background!

Lachlan shook his head and said lightly to Fred, 'My plans altered. But I could never forget the folk around here that I grew up with, I assure you, Fred.'

'Aye, well…have you come back for good?'

'I hope so, Fred, for the time being at least. I'm going to be working with Dr Christa.'

Fred grinned, showing a mouth missing several teeth. 'She's well worth coming back for, a bonny lass like her! You're a lucky young blighter, aren't you?'

'Hush, Fred!' admonished Bessie. 'You let your tongue run away with you.' She smiled at the two doctors. 'Now, I'm going to get us some tea and a little bit of the shortbread you like while you look at Fred, Dr Christa.'

'A cup of tea would be lovely, Bessie.' Christa sat down beside Fred. 'Right, Fred, first of all, what have you been up to with your hand?'

Fred looked down at his bandaged hand as if he'd forgotten about it. 'This? Och, that nurse of yours did it up for me, but she's always fussing about. I cut it on a piece of glass when I was pouring myself a wee dram. The tumbler fell out of my hand and I fell, trying to pick it up.'

Christa took his gnarled old hand in hers, and undid the bandage. His fingers were misshapen with arthritis, but what worried her was the palm of his hand, swollen and red, with the danger that the infection might spread, leading to septicaemia.

'Lorna was worried that it might be infected, Fred, and I'm afraid she's right. You'll need antibiotics, and it's most important that you finish the course. I want you to take one tablet four times a day. Lorna will come in tomorrow to see how it's going on.'

The old man frowned and repeated slowly, 'One tablet four times a day? How can I do that? If I've taken the tablet I can't retake it!'

Christa laughed. 'You're right, Fred, I put it badly. I should have said take *a* tablet four times a day…'

Fred winked up at Lachlan. 'You've got to watch these lasses—she's trying to make out I'm doolally!'

'I'll put these tablets in the box divided up into sections for each day with all your heart pills.'

'I'll be like a rattle when I've finished,' Fred grumbled.

'Talking of food, Bessie says you haven't eaten today.'

Fred waved an irritable hand at her. 'Stop fussing, woman! Bessie's trying to force-feed me, and I'm not hungry.'

'And it's none too warm in here,' said Lachlan, going to the door. 'You need some more peat on that fire, and I'm going to get some. I bet there's some already cut outside.'

Christa watched him go out and reflected that Lachlan Maguire had hidden depths. When she'd first encountered him he'd seemed brusque and impatient, and she would never have imagined he would have been the thoughtful and kindly man he appeared to be now with the Logans.

She took out her sphygmomanometer and stethoscope out of her bag, and started to check Fred's blood pressure, and then listened to his heart. As she'd expected, it sounded erratic and fast, labouring to circulate the blood round his body.

'Well, how is it?' demanded Fred. 'I'll bet it's racing with a lass like you so near me!'

'You're a wicked old man, Fred.' Christa laughed, putting away her stethoscope. 'But I really wish that you'd let us get you both a little bit of help—someone just to come in for a few minutes a day to give you a hand with things. It would help Bessie, you know,' she added craftily.

Fred scowled. 'Has my lad Ian put you up to this? He wants us near him in Inverness, but I'm not bothering them. Anyway,' he added half-humorously, 'my daughter-in-law's a real tyrant—I don't fancy being in her hands!'

Christa knelt down beside him, took his gnarled old hand in hers, looking into the faded blue eyes, and said gently, 'They're worried about you both being so isolated, Fred—we all are. Won't you try it for a little while, please?'

The old man sighed. 'Aye, lass, perhaps you're right. The two of us are getting no younger. I'm a stubborn old fellow, I know. But if you think Bessie needs help then you can go ahead and organise it—but just for a wee while, to tide us over.'

Lachlan appeared with a box of peat sods and put one of them on the fire, where it hissed and sent up a spiral of aromatic smoke.

'I see you've lost a few tiles from your roof, Fred,' he said. 'The winter's coming on and you ought to have them looked at.'

'Aye. I'll do it when I've time, lad.'

Lachlan laughed. 'I wasn't suggesting you should do it. I've got a builder coming to Ardenleigh and I'll send him up to do them for you.' He put his hand up to stop Fred's protest. 'And before you say anything, that's doctor's orders!'

Fred subsided back in his chair and shrugged. 'You're bullies, all of you!' he said gruffly, but Christa felt there was a certain relief in his manner, as if he'd realised that it wasn't such a bad thing to accept help—if only for Bessie's sake.

Bessie reappeared and handed round cups of tea in pretty little cups of bone china and a plate with warm shortbread covered with sugar. She wouldn't let Christa help her pour out the tea or distribute the food—however frail, she was determined to show the doctors that they could do things independently. Despite Fred submitting to help, it was going to be difficult for them to accept that someone would be coming in every day to keep an eye on them. They were so used to doing everything for themselves.

'When Lorna comes in tomorrow morning to look at your hand, she'll introduce you to the home help she'll put in place,' Christa explained. 'She's such a nice young girl and will do any shopping for you once a week—and if you need the bed changed or perhaps a casserole done, she'll do that for you…'

Bessie stood up and said indignantly, 'I certainly don't need anyone cooking for us—I hope I can still put a hotpot in the oven!'

'Consider yourself told off!' remarked Lachlan with a grin as they left.

The car did its usual impression of a bucking bronco as they set off again towards the valley below the Logans' cottage, a rough, grinding noise coming from the engine.

Lachlan raised his eyebrows. 'It really might be a good idea to get this car serviced soon. It sounds very dodgy to me.'

'Oh, don't fuss, it'll be fine. It's never let me down yet.'

Christa put her foot on the accelerator and the car seemed to recover for a few miles, but after a renewed series of bangs inside the engine and one or two lurches it came to an abrupt halt.

They both sat in stunned silence for a second, then Lachlan laughed, 'Never let you down, eh?'

'It's Sod's law, isn't it? Blast the thing! Are you any good at mending engines?'

'I can have a go, but on the whole I'm more au fait with the human body. You'd better ring your rescue company.'

Christa scrabbled for her phone and scrolled down to the number. After a few seconds she looked at him quizzically. 'No signal,' she reported.

'I'd better have a look at its innards, then.' Lachlan climbed out of the car and opened the bonnet, peering into it with a frown, then scratched his head. 'As I said, I'm more familiar with human intestines than all these pipes and tubes in a car. Perhaps,' he said hopefully, 'the plugs need cleaning.'

He delved into the engine, took out the plugs and began cleaning them with his handkerchief, then examined the oil and water levels.

'See if that brings it back to life,' he said.

Christa turned the key. There was a spasmodic cough and a brief shaking, then silence.

'I don't seem to have cured it,' remarked Lachlan. 'We'll have to wait until someone comes along, I suppose.' He looked up at the Logans' cottage, high above them on a hill and the little spiral of smoke drifting over the roof. 'I could run back there and use their land line,' he suggested.

'It's miles away, and I'm sure someone will come along soon.' Christa gave an exasperated sigh. 'I should have had the thing serviced, I know—there just didn't seem to be a window of time, what with organising the funeral and trying to get a locum…' She flicked a guilty look at Lachlan. 'Sorry, I'm certainly not moaning about organising Isobel's funeral. It's just—'

'I know,' he said abruptly. 'It must have been difficult, and of course I'm very grateful to you.' He was silent for a second, looking down at the road, scuffing the dirt with his shoes, then he said roughly, 'Of course I should have been there to do that. If I'd known earlier that she'd died…'

'We tried to find you—her solicitor did his best. If you'd left a forwarding address…'

Was it guilt that made his expression change

and harden? Whatever it was, Christa had touched a raw nerve. 'Well, I didn't leave a forwarding address,' he said tersely. 'It's too complicated to go into now, but if my mother hadn't been so damn selfish…'

Christa stared at him in surprise. How could he say that about his mother? Surely she had been the most gentle and kindly of people and not deserving the cold-shoulder treatment meted out by her son.

'Aren't you being rather harsh on Isobel?' she said coldly.

Lachlan scowled. 'You don't know the circumstances—you see her as a colleague, not as a mother who ruined her son's life!'

There was a shocked silence broken only by the bleating of sheep in a field across the valley.

'What on earth do you mean?' asked Christa bluntly. 'How the hell did she ruin your life? Isn't this all rather melodramatic? After all, you've had a good job in a wonderful country—all you had to do was send the odd e-mail…'

'Don't tell me what I should have done, please.' His blue eyes glared icily at her. 'I don't need lessons in how to be a good son. It's too late for that.'

Funny how the atmosphere between them had plummeted yet again in the space of half an hour! God, he was touchy! But, then, she might have known that someone like him wouldn't have taken the slightest hint of criticism. How typical that was of a man—from charming and gentle to hostile and angry!

'For God's sake, stop feeling sorry for yourself,' she snapped. 'It seems to me you punished a lovely, kind woman for no good reason!'

Steely blue eyes held hers. 'Then let me tell you the reason that I left this "lovely, kind woman", as you call her…' Lachlan's voice grated with emotion. 'I was seventeen when I learned that my mother—the woman I looked up to and revered—had been having an affair, betrayed my father and me!'

Christa's jaw dropped and she stared at him in disbelief. 'Isobel had an affair?' she faltered. 'I can hardly believe it!'

'My father was not an easy man, he had a quick temper, but he was devastated. She refused to end the affair, and he left. The happy home life I'd thought we'd had vanished. I couldn't believe a word she said and it was as if the family had never been happy, never been a unit at all. She had put her own selfish desires before that of her young son.'

Christa was stunned into silence then said slowly, 'I never knew that. She never talked about her life before I came—just the odd remark about you and how well you'd done at med school.'

'Then,' he said bitingly, 'you had no right to tell me what I should or should not have done—you didn't know the background. Just because you forged a close bond with my mother, it doesn't mean to say that she was an angel.'

'I'm surprised you came back at all if that is how you think of her.' Christa glared at his mutinous face. 'Perhaps it was only the fact that the practice became available—is that it?'

'How dare you say that?' His voice was low and controlled but she could see the fury in his face. 'I came back because I loved my mother…'

Christa closed her eyes. 'Oh, God, I'm sorry,

I shouldn't have said that. I didn't mean to hurt you. Of course you loved her.' As usual, she'd opened her big mouth before thinking.

Lachlan pushed a hand through his hair wearily and kicked a stone roughly into the verge. 'Oh, what the hell, it's I who should be sorry,' he said quietly. 'I've been unforgivably rude—perhaps it's because I feel so guilty. Of course I regret like mad not being here when she died, not making my peace with her.'

Suddenly he looked worn and tired, something grief-stricken in his eyes as he gazed unseeingly over the valley, and Christa glimpsed something of his inner turmoil.

She looked at him quizzically and said gently, 'We seem to be apologising to each other rather a lot! Let's hope our working relationship goes more smoothly.'

'Of course it will,' he said firmly. 'I know we can work well together. I suppose I've still not come to terms with things.' He sighed, a sudden sweet smile lighting his face. 'Friends again, then?'

And because he looked so gorgeous and incredibly sad, Christa forgave him, pushing to the back of her mind that she could never have left her own mother in similar circumstances. She smiled back at him, putting her hand up to pat his cheek comfortingly. 'Of course we'll be friends,' she said gently.

He caught her hand and squeezed it. 'Friendly colleagues, a good idea,' he murmured.

CHAPTER FOUR

A GUST OF wind with a cold bite to it swirled around them, and a last bright shaft of light from the sun made the loch glitter. The blue skies were disappearing and dark clouds were coming up fast over the hills, changing the scene very quickly from benign to a dramatic, brooding intensity. Christa shivered and hugged her arms round her body, and Lachlan took off his jacket and put it around Christa's shoulders.

'Hey, you're cold. Look, put this jacket on.'

'I don't need it, I'm fine!'

He pulled the jacket round her and said firmly, 'You're not fine, you've gone blue! I don't want you going down with pneumonia before I've even joined the workforce.'

'I'm made of hardier stuff than that!' she protested.

He pulled the jacket further around her. 'Listen

to me—I'm a doctor. I can tell when someone's getting hypothermia without having to take their core temperature.'

Lachlan's blue eyes danced mischievously into hers, and Christa looked away hastily. She wanted to be friends with him—but not too friendly! She stepped away from him, confused by her mixed emotions. One minute she was enraged by him and his plans to raise money for the house, and the next minute she was filled with sympathy because he obviously felt the loss of his mother so acutely, and the fact he'd missed her funeral. And now he was flirting with her. It was like being on a roller-coaster!

Lachlan's sexiness and cheeky smile, and the nearness of him, triggered a powerful memory of how it had been when Colin had been near her. She felt a longing to be held and loved again. In her imagination she could almost feel Lachlan's demanding firm mouth on hers, passionate, urgent, and his muscular body crushing her close to him. A little trail of fire ripped through her body, and for a second she closed her eyes, leaning provocatively towards him. That long-forgotten sensation of desire flickered through her again, bitter-sweet.

She couldn't encourage him like this—hadn't they just agreed they'd be 'friendly colleagues'? She stepped back from Lachlan abruptly and gave an involuntary shiver as if, having stepped to the brink of an abyss, she'd saved herself in the nick of time.

'There you are!' he said triumphantly. 'You're shivering. I know you're freezing!'

She looked at him mock-sternly, trying to keep things on a light level. She had to make it clear once again that their friendship was to be a strictly business arrangement, with positively no flirting! Wasn't that how her relationship with Colin had started—a little mild flirting?

'I'm actually feeling quite warm.' She smiled, shrugging off the jacket he'd put around her shoulders and handing it back to him. 'If you live around here long enough you become quite tough.'

'I think I guessed that…' He grinned down at her. 'I knew from the moment I first saw you yesterday that you were one feisty girl.'

'What on earth makes you think that?'

'Oh, I've gleaned quite a bit of knowledge over the past twenty-four hours to realise that you're something very special.'

Those blue eyes were flirting with her again, and she bit her lip. It could be Colin speaking, just the kind of thing he would say, and she was damned if she'd be hoodwinked by that any more! There was something chancy about Lachlan Maguire when he wasn't in a sombre mood, she concluded—that teasing manner combined with eye-catching looks spelt danger with a capital D!

She shook her head and said in a brisk, no-nonsense voice, 'You don't know me at all—just as I know nothing about you. It's going to be a learning process for both of us over the next few months, and I'm looking forward to a very good friendly working relationship from now on.'

A smiled touched Lachlan's lips at her formal tone and the slight emphasis she'd put on the word 'working'.

'Of course,' he said urbanely with a little bow of his head.

Perhaps, thought Christa nervously, the penny would drop now that she was only interested in him as a colleague and nothing else—no dangerous flirting! She stole a glance at him, his long, lean body now leaning against the car and his thick hair being blown casually over his forehead. Yes, it was definitely safer to make it quite plain from the outset that their relationship had to be purely professional—friendly maybe, but purely professional!

The sound of a car changing gear as it came up the steep hill floated towards them, and Christa went to the other side of the road to wave it down. Lachlan watched her wryly. They'd crossed swords twice in one afternoon, but he knew there was a spark between them. How sensible, then, that they'd agreed to be friendly colleagues and nothing more—keep that spark at a distance!

Of course it was a relief to him that their relationship should stay at that level, he thought. The truth was that he deeply resented the fact that his mother should try and manipulate his life even from the grave—how dared she suggest he marry Christa Lennox just because she'd formed a close bond with the girl? How did Isobel know the kind of girl he wanted?

In another time and place perhaps Christa would have been the sort of girl he would have gone for. He sighed. And if she hadn't been Angus Lennox's niece... But that was a subject he was better off keeping to himself.

'So this guy's on top of the roof and I'm shouting at him to come down—and guess who he turns out to be?'

Christa and her mother, Pat, were sitting in Pat's little bright kitchen, having a quick cup of coffee before Christa went back to afternoon surgery. Titan was lying contentedly by a radiator, half-asleep. Christa cradled her mug of coffee in her hand and her mother leaned forward, her bright, dark eyes, so like Christa's, alive with interest.

'I can't imagine who it would be. Brad Pitt perhaps?'

Christa laughed. 'I wish! Of all people, he's Isobel's son. Lachlan Maguire!'

Pat Lennox stared at Christa in astonishment. 'Isobel's son?' she repeated. 'Lachlan Maguire? He's turned up, after all this time—I never thought we'd see him again!'

'I know—it's incredible, isn't it? He didn't know Isobel had died until after the funeral. He's been working in Australia.'

'But what was he doing on top of the roof?'

'That's what I wondered. I thought he was filching lead, but it turns out he was just inspecting the guttering. The place is very neglected, and his mother's left it to him. You do remember him, then?'

Pat took a sip of coffee and replaced the mug precisely on a mat on the table. 'Yes,' she said rather abruptly. 'Of course I remember him—he used to run home through the village from school, and your father supplied any drugs the practice needed.'

'Well, as I said in my text to you on Sunday, explaining that I wouldn't be able to pop in and see you, there was an incident with two youths in the big barn and luckily he was there to help.'

Pat got up from the table and went over to the

coffee jug, her back to Christa. 'Sounds as if he came in the nick of time. Another cup of coffee? I'm having one…' Her voice was light, inconsequential, and she turned back to Christa with a bright smile. 'Fancy him being found. Sad that he missed Isobel's funeral, though. How long's he going to be here?'

'That's the thing, he's decided to leave Australia and he's going to come back to the practice. At first I wasn't sure about it but, actually, it's a relief that I've got someone.'

'You mean he's going to be working with you?'

'Well, yes. Apparently he's been pining for Scotland.'

'Did…did he say why he left, or at least stayed away for so long?'

'It's extraordinary—he told me he found out when he was just about to leave school that Isobel had had an affair when he was younger. That's why his father left. Lachlan blamed his mother for the break-up of the family, and I guess that's why he and she had a falling out. He didn't go into detail.'

Pat put her hands round her coffee mug as

if to warm them, and gazed ahead of her as if looking into the past.

'But that was many years ago...' she said softly, and shook her head. 'All this time and never a word from him.' She focussed back on Christa. 'You'll be working closely with him, then, won't you? Probably get to know him quite well.'

A little nervous tremor passed through Christa, the doubts she was having about not allowing herself to get too involved with this man surfacing yet again.

She shrugged, trying to appear casually indifferent. 'Well, as colleagues we're bound to see each other quite a lot.' She looked at her mother more closely. 'You OK, Mum? You look a little pale.'

Pat Lennox stood up and moved restlessly to the window, twisting her hands together. 'I'm fine... It's just, well, you seem to be irretrievably bound up with the Maguire family, always working with them. Couldn't you get someone else... someone who has nothing to do with them?'

Christa looked taken aback. 'But surely you liked Isobel, Mum?'

Pat's lips compressed slightly and she said briefly, 'She offered you a job near me when I was very ill, and I was grateful for that—although perhaps I didn't find her as…congenial as you did.'

'I never knew you thought that,' said Christa in some surprise.

Pat picked up the mugs and stacked them in the dishwasher, then shrugged. 'It's of no consequence—one can't like everybody,' she said offhandedly. 'Tell me, is Lachlan's family going to join him soon?'

'Oh, he's no wife or children…and he can start straight away, thank goodness. Frankly, I'm finding it pretty hard going at the moment and I can't wait for him to start properly next Monday.'

Pat turned round, leaning against the machine, her eyes studying Christa intently. 'You will be careful, won't you, darling, working closely with another single man…?'

Christa laughed. 'Oh, for goodness' sake,

Mum. Just because I fell for that rat Colin when he was working at the practice, it doesn't mean that every single man I work with is going to break my heart! I'll be extremely careful who I fall for another time. I've learned my lesson. He may be reasonably good looking and have a bit of charm, but it's mixed with a short fuse. No—it'll be strictly business from now on, I can assure you.'

She met her mother's searching look almost defiantly, because she meant every word, thought Christa fiercely. She'd made it clear to Lachlan the other day when the car had broken down that there was no way she would allow relationships to get in the way of work. Yes, she admitted he was one sexy guy and that kiss had set every erogenous zone in her body buzzing and kept coming back to haunt her. But liaisons of any sort with him were quite definitely not on the cards. Once bitten, twice shy.

'Well, if you're happy to be working with Lachlan and he's a good doctor, I guess that's fine.' There was a terse note in Pat's voice and she softened it by smiling down at Christa lovingly. 'I…I just don't want you hurt again, darling, that's all.' She paused and sighed. 'What I really want is for you to meet a nice reliable man who won't let you down.'

Christa got up and gave her mother a hug, grinning. 'God, you sound as if you want me to marry Mr Dull-as-Ditchwater… Anyway, you're looking very glam today—I like that tweed jacket. Are you off somewhere exciting?'

Pat laughed, suddenly looking very like her daughter, although her hair was white now.

'If you call going out with Bertie to the pub outside the village for a meal exciting!'

'Good for you!' Christa looked teasingly at her mother. 'You know, I don't know why you and Bertie Smith don't move in together—he only lives in the next flat. You might as well be married!'

'Oh, no, I value my independence too much. Besides…' Her mother's voice was brisk, devoid of self-pity. 'The thing is, I'm very fond of Bertie, but I made one lot of vows once, and I'm not inclined to make the same ones again.' She glanced at the kitchen clock on the wall. 'Aren't you going to be late? It's nearly two o'clock.'

'Oh, God, you're right…I'll have to fly!' Christa blew a kiss to her mother as she dashed out. 'See you soon—enjoy your meal… Come on, Titan, back to work!'

Friday night and a chance to wind down in the local little gym after a gruelling week. The surgery seemed to have been crammed with patients needing urgent referrals, and more than the usual amount of visits, and however ambivalent Christa was about Lachlan joining the practice, she couldn't wait for him to start work on Monday and take some of the load from her.

She really enjoyed her weekly workout at the gym, which her friend Richie had converted from one of the little warehouses off the main road. She admired Richie so much—he had been a ski instructor in the Cairngorms during the winter, but after a bad accident had had to give that up. After that he had trained to become a personal trainer, and had set up this small business. Gradually he was building up his clientele.

'Now a final exercise for those abdominals!' he shouted. 'Touching the floor with the heels as you air-bicycle for twenty… Good, good—and stop! Now a good stretch against the bars and then you can put the kettle on!'

Eight pairs of legs collapsed back on the floor and there was a general gasp of relief.

'You worked us hard tonight, Richie,' protested Christa, wiping her forehead. 'I'm so out of condition!'

'That's because you've missed a few weeks,' said Richie mock-sternly. 'I know you've been run off your feet, but no excuses now because I hear you've Isobel's son to help!'

'Yes, thank God. He starts properly on Monday—such a relief.' She smiled at Richie and looked around the gym, which seemed quite crowded. 'You seem to have more people here since I was here last. Things going well?'

Richie pulled a face and rotated his hands. 'So, so. At the moment I feel I'm just about making a breakthrough. But I've heard rumours about a new development…'

'When did you hear that?' asked Christa,

amazed that what had apparently just been an idea of Lachlan's should be almost common knowledge so quickly. Hard to keep any secrets in a small place like Errin Bridge!

'The builder who adapted this place for me said that all the land around your medical centre could be sold off for a leisure centre and holiday complex, even a golf course! Can you imagine what that could do to a little place like this? I've invested quite a bit of money in it…' His voice trailed off, but Christa got his drift.

She looked at Richie's worried face with concern. 'It's not set in stone, is it, though?'

'Hopefully not. But I couldn't possibly compete with that sort of thing so close.' He sighed heavily. 'It's not something I want to think about, especially now Ruth is expecting our first baby.'

Christa was filled with sympathy for a guy who had tried so hard to turn his life round after his accident and the numerous operations he'd had to mend his hips. She tried to think of some positives. 'But surely that sort of place would be much more expensive than coming here. The subs would be huge.'

Richie shrugged. 'I've no doubt they'd hold out a carrot for a special opening offer. Anyway…' he straightened his shoulders and gave a wan smile '…I'm damned if I'll give in—I'll just have to try and attract more people somehow!'

'Good for you, Richie. I'll certainly try and get my friends to come, and some of my patients could definitely do with the exercise! It may never happen anyway.'

Christa went into the changing room, feeling slightly depressed for Richie and more than ever determined to try and convince Lachlan that his plans could adversely affect a great many people in the village.

She slung her old warm jacket over her shoulders and changed her shoes, deciding that she'd have a shower at home as there was a queue to use it in the cloakroom. She flicked a look at herself in the mirror and pulled a face—hair like a bird's nest and a face like a tomato! What a marked contrast to the photos round the walls of various celebrities apparently having just finished a punishing routine and looking neat and glowing.

Alice, one of the practice receptionists, had also been to the class. She saw Christa glancing at the photos and grinned. 'There's been a bit of airbrushing on those photos! How else do you think the girls in keep-fit DVDs manage to look so cool and glamorous after forty minutes' punishment without some digital tweaking?'

'I need more than digital tweaking.' Christa laughed. 'I just want to get home before anyone sees me in this disgusting state. See you on Monday.'

She pushed through the door and barged heavily into the muscular arms of a tall guy walking past.

'Whoa, there! In a hurry?' The man held her at arm's length, then raised his eyebrows in surprise. 'Well, hello there! Dr Lennox, I presume. Getting your stress levels down?'

Lachlan Maguire was looking down at her with amused eyes, and she got a quick impression of a strapping, well-honed, muscular figure in Lycra shorts.

'Something like that,' she gulped, making a

grab at her coat to conceal her perspiring, out-of-condition body.

The coat slipped from her shoulders onto the floor, and she stood before him feeling hot, dishevelled and purple-faced. She tried to disregard the fact that in gym attire Lachlan Maguire was the sexiest man that she'd ever seen.

'What are you doing here?' she enquired, trying to control her ragged breathing to something slower than if she'd been running a marathon.

'Trying to keep in good condition, like you!' Lachlan said, his eyes twinkling as they swept over her beetroot face. 'You've obviously upped your heart rate—keeping your body in good shape!'

Christa wasn't sure if there was a double meaning to his remark. Was he referring to her admirable training regime or was he being more personal?

'I try to keep healthy,' she rejoined.

'I approve of that.'

He stepped onto the treadmill and started off at a brisk jogging level on tanned muscular legs, grinning cheerfully at her as he settled into a steady rhythm, increasing to a faster pace with seemingly little effort.

Christa clutched her coat firmly round her top. 'I thought you might be coming to suss out the competition,' she said lightly, mindful of their mutual pact to be friendly colleagues.

He flicked a puzzled look at her then his face cleared. 'Oh, you mean the leisure centre? I told you, it's only an idea yet.' He added rather offhandedly, 'But I don't suppose what I have in mind would have any effect on this place. I imagine we'd attract different clientele.'

'In what way? You'd be offering fitness classes and machine work. Where's the difference?'

He shrugged, still pounding away easily on the machine and scarcely out of breath. 'I imagine this gym would be cheaper and with less commitment. Here you can just pop in without joining for a minimum time…'

'But you can see how it would compete directly with Richie's little business.'

'I don't agree—I don't think he's got anything to worry about.'

Christa warmed to her theme. 'And what about

the local people who benefit by Richie's gym—all the people popping into the little café over the road for lunch after they've exercised? I bet you'll have a plush coffee place under the same roof.'

Lachlan decreased his speed and stopped the machine, before jumping off, barely panting and breathing with remarkable ease. He put out his hand and brushed some of Christa's dishevelled hair from her forehead, his eyes travelling down to her cleavage where a little bead of perspiration was making its way between her breasts.

'For God's sake.' He grinned. 'You're in headmistress mode again! If I did go ahead—and I repeat "if",' there's plenty of room for both businesses and more jobs to spread around as well.'

Then he got onto the rowing machine and started rowing with powerful strokes that looked effortless. He was the picture of athleticism, the merest sheen of perspiration on his forehead. The Australian way of life had obviously suited him, thought Christa, aware that she was still puffing and out of breath from her exercise class.

She dragged her eyes away from his impressive physique and said in her most reasonable voice, 'But it'll change the whole character of the village. Don't you agree?'

'Not sure I do,' he said lightly, upping the speed of his rowing.

Christa gave a snort of exasperation and stood looking at him with her arms folded. He stopped rowing and got off the machine.

'Got another point to make about the gym?' he asked impishly.

She shrugged. 'No—I've said all I want to about that, for the moment!' She turned to go out then stopped. 'Oh, by the way, I forgot that I haven't shown you your room at the surgery yet. If you come round tomorrow morning at about 11 o'clock I'll show it to you and give you a rundown on the computer system.'

Lachlan nodded. 'Good idea. I'll be there.'

He watched her as she marched out of the door, and grinned to himself. Little Miss Bossy, he thought, but, wow, what a figure, and how bloody sexy she looked in that far-too-tight Lycra costume! It was rather a pity that he'd sort of promised not to be anything but a friendly colleague, because he was going to find Christa's proximity extremely tempting...although, of course, just because his mother had said he should marry the girl made Christa the last person on earth he'd ever have an affair with. It was out of the question.

'So this is it. It was your mother's room, and we haven't really had a chance to clear it yet, but perhaps you're the one who ought to sift through things anyway.'

Christa watched Lachlan as he walked to the window, pulling aside the blinds and looking at the view. Then he turned back, surveying the room rather bleakly. That familiar fleeting expression of great sadness crossed his face and there was almost a little-boy-lost look about him. Suddenly Christa's arms ached to go round him, to comfort him, let him know that he wasn't alone in his grief.

At last he said haltingly, 'So this is where my mother worked, until about three weeks ago. It feels...rather weird.'

Christa said gently, 'It must do. No doubt you

want to look at things quietly for a while. When you've finished, come through to the office.'

Lachlan nodded and sat down. The room was neat and tidy, very different from the house—it was almost as if this had been Isobel's real home, where she liked to be best. On the wall facing the examination bed was a large painting of the view over the hills from Errin Bridge—the sun was shining on heather-covered hills and the sparkle of the loch could be seen in the distance. He smiled. He knew that view so well, and he could guess just why she'd put it in that spot—so that nervous patients could look at it and be calmed.

He opened the drawers of the desk—they were empty except for a few papers and a brown envelope with some photos inside. He pulled them out and took a deep breath, staring at them as if transfixed. They showed a boy at various stages of his life—a toddler on a little tricycle, a young lad grinning into the camera with fishing rods in his hand, and a teenager with a sullen expression. They were all of him and written across the back of each were the words 'My darling son'.

Lachlan closed his eyes for a moment, overcome, then he put the photos back neatly in the drawer. The love he'd felt for his mother surged over him again and he felt torn by conflicting emotions—almost reluctant to accept his mother's legacy of the house if he could not in his own mind make amends in his heart by trying to fulfil her wishes.

'But you don't own me, Mum,' he muttered. 'You can't tell me who I must marry just because you liked Christa Lennox…'

CHAPTER FIVE

IT WAS THE weekly practice meeting, made more important because it was Lachlan's first official day at work. He came into the room chatting to Lorna, the community nurse, and Sarah Duthey, the part-time practice nurse, whom he had met the week before. Christa was standing by the coffee machine, reading through the agenda.

'Are you coming or going?' enquired Lachlan, noting she was still in her warm overcoat.

She looked up at him and dragged in her breath, swallowing hard. Holy Moses, he looked drop-dead gorgeous! Until now she'd seen him in a variety of casual clothes, from shorts to ragged jeans, but today he was in a dark, well cut suit and crisp white shirt, which seemed to emphasise his tanned skin and rangy figure. He looked confident, relaxed and as if he could run the health service singlehanded. Brad Pitt, eat your heart out, she thought wryly.

She tried to ignore the double thump of her heartbeat, and said smilingly, 'I've just got back from taking Titan for a walk. He had a bust-up with a dog twice his size and it took ages to catch him, so I've only just arrived.' She waved a mug at him. 'What about a coffee?' she asked.

'That's a great idea. I haven't had any breakfast yet—the kettle went on the blink and I forgot to stock up on milk…'

Christa smiled sympathetically and pushed some biscuits towards him. 'Perhaps these will help.'

'Thanks, they'll certainly keep me going.' He raised his coffee mug as if it were a wine glass and grinned at her. 'Well, here's to the first day of a happy working relationship!'

'I'll drink to that! By the way, before I forget, I'm having the director of information technology, Ahmed Kumar, round for supper on Thursday evening, and he wants to meet you. It's just a general discussion about networking the computer systems within the local hospitals and GP practices—not wildly exciting, I'm afraid.'

He grinned. 'On the contrary, fascinating stuff! No, seriously, I'm keen to be in on that, but more importantly a cooked meal would be a lifesaver! I seem to be on a restricted diet at the moment of a lot of ready meals in the microwave. It would be great to have some proper good food. It'll be the highlight of my week!'

'Don't be expecting a cordon bleu experience,' Christa warned nervously, suddenly wondering if her invitation for a meal was such a good idea.

Then Ben Conlan, the practice manager, came in and Christa introduced him to Lachlan. Ben had been on holiday for the past two weeks and hadn't met Lachlan before. He was a harassed-looking man who had a demanding wife and two sullen teenage children. Sometimes Christa thought he came in early and stayed late to get away from his family!

'How was the holiday, Ben?' she asked.

He groaned. 'We spent two weeks prising the kids out of nightclubs late at night, or going round the resort trying to find them, wondering what they were getting up to. I tell you, I'm glad to be back at work!'

They all laughed, and even Ben smiled. 'Good to meet you,' he said to Lachlan. 'We were all so fond of Isobel and it's great to know that you're carrying on the family tradition. I'm afraid my holiday came at totally the wrong moment, leaving Christa to try and find a replacement, so I'm so pleased that you arrived in the nick of time.'

Lachlan smiled around pleasantly at them all. 'I'm glad to be here. My mother obviously had a place in everyone's hearts at the practice, and I hope I'll be able to fill her shoes adequately and that I can give good service in Errin Bridge. However…' He paused for a second and the others looked at him questioningly. 'I have to say I'm a little dismayed at the state of the place—no need to point it out really…'

'You're right,' agreed Ben. 'Isobel had finally agreed to at least do up this part of the building that housed the practice, but sadly she died before we could get around to it.'

'Well, I intend to put things right. I'm planning

to have the place reroofed ASAP, and when I've got the money together to do the rest.'

'Word's got out about your plans to sell some of the land for a leisure and holiday centre,' admitted Ben, adding cautiously, 'If the plans go through, I can imagine there'd be quite a lot of interest.'

Lachlan grinned. 'I'll have to be careful of any secrets I have in future! Why, I hardly know what the plans are myself yet!'

Christa bit her lip—better not to stir up a hornet's nest at Lachlan's first meeting.

Then, as usual at the meetings, there were discussions about the budget, and individual patients and those who were housebound and had special needs.

Lorna, the district nurse, a pleasant-faced, motherly woman, explained to Lachlan how she and another community nurse in the area took it in turns to see their more outlying patients and that there was a rapid response team to step in for emergency care. Once a week a minor surgery clinic at the local cottage hospital offered treatment for removal of warts and moles and the different GP surgeries in the area took it in turns to man it.

'It's supposed to be for minor surgery,' said Christa, 'although some of the patients use us as a drop-in centre for a good chat! But it does have an X-ray unit and other back-up.'

'I'm all for that,' said Lachlan enthusiastically. 'Having worked in the Flying Doctor service I've got used to spreading myself over the whole area and not being confined to one surgery—keeps you in touch with the hospital as well. And I can tell you I'll be pleased not to work in forty-degree temperatures!'

Christa had a sudden image of Lachlan in shorts and a bush hat, leaping on and off aeroplanes and striding out with boundless energy over the Outback to get to his remote patients. It was rather an exciting thought…

Lorna's voice cut into Christa's reverie. 'Then I'll put Lachlan down for next week's stint, shall I?' she asked. 'I should think Christa could do with a break!'

'I look forward to it—I want to get into the swing of things as quickly as possible.'

Ben put his hand up. 'Just before we break up the meeting, don't forget the village dance next month to raise money for the new scanner at St Luke's. I said we'd take a party from the practice, so put it in your diaries. And I expect everyone to come!'

He looked sternly at them all, and Lorna giggled. 'Is it a three-line whip, then?'

Christa's heart skipped a beat. Every year the village held a dance for a good cause. Two years ago she'd been with Colin, and that had been the night that he'd told her their affair was over. It didn't hold good memories for her, and even if she wanted to go there didn't seem anyone to go with. Unless… She flicked a quick look at Lachlan, lounging back in his chair and making notes, and looking incredibly dishy. Then she dismissed the notion as preposterous!

Her thoughts were interrupted by Ginny Calder putting her head round the door.

'Could one of the doctors come immediately? We've a young girl who's just come in, and I think she needs to be seen urgently. Her name's not on our list—she wouldn't give me any details anyway.'

Lorna grinned. 'Well, Lachlan, you wanted to get into the swing of things! Looks like your wish is going to be fulfilled. Do you want to take this one?'

Lachlan stood up. 'No time like the present,' he remarked. 'Would you bring her into my room, Ginny?'

She was only a kid, Lachlan thought, and very heavily pregnant. She slumped into the chair and bent over tiredly, allowing for the bulge of the baby. Lachlan ran a quick assessing eye over her—matted hair, dishevelled clothing and a greyish complexion. She looked uncared for, young and vulnerable.

He bent down beside her, noting that close to she looked even younger than he'd thought.

'Aren't you feeling well?' he asked gently.

'I feel dizzy,' she mumbled. 'Not myself. Weak, sort of…'

He looked at her thin face and stick-like legs. 'Have you had anything to eat today?'

'A bit of toast…'

'Well, let me just take a few details.'

A guarded look crossed the girl's face. 'What d'you want to know?' she muttered sullenly. 'I just want a bit of medicine—a pick-me-up.'

Lachlan guessed that it had only been because she felt so ill that she'd come to the surgery at all, and that she wanted to remain as anonymous as possible. He'd make a safe bet that she'd never been to an antenatal clinic or had any tests done.

'Look, it's only for our records. No one else will know,' he assured her gently. 'Your age and where you live. To start with, what's your name?'

'Lindsay Cooper,' was the muttered reply.

'And your age?'

She looked at him defiantly. 'Fifteen… And don't tell me to get rid of the baby,' she said fiercely. 'If I went home they'd make me have an abortion, and I won't do that.' She stared at Lachlan as if daring him to censure her.

Lachlan's face was impassive as he wrote down the information. 'Then we'll make sure you and your baby have all the support you need,' he reassured her.

Lindsay was a tough little cookie, he reckoned, noting the flash of obstinacy in her eyes. She wasn't about to be pushed around by anybody imposing their wishes on her.

'And do you live locally?'

'I'm…I'm living temporary, like…with an aunt. She doesn't know I've come.' Then more belligerently, 'And I don't want anyone to know either.'

From that Lachlan surmised that the young girl's family had not been supportive of her condition.

'OK…can you tell me how many months pregnant you are?'

Lindsay shrugged. 'Not sure…a few months maybe.'

'Never mind—I can make a rough assessment and you can have a scan later. I'd like to take your blood pressure and get some blood from you. But I've got a pretty good idea why you're feeling so dizzy.'

He took her hand in his, holding it palm down. The nails were cracked and spoon-shaped, and together with her red-rimmed eyes were reliable signs of iron deficiency. No wonder she felt so exhausted.

She looked suspiciously at Lachlan as he started to wind a sphygmomanometer cuff round her arm, propping up the scale indicator on the cupboard by the bed. He watched the dial as he pumped air into the tube, and made a note of the result without comment, then leaned back in his chair and looked at her kindly. ‘I think you need building up, and a course of iron tablets. And bed rest wouldn’t come amiss either.’

Lindsay laughed scornfully. ‘I won’t get much of that at my auntie’s. I have to give my bed up in the daytime to her daughter who works nights at an old folks’ home, and there’s four little ones running around all day.’

‘I was thinking perhaps a few days’ rest in the local hospital—just to keep a check on you and a scan to discover how many months you are. How about that?’

The girl started to protest, but in a muted way. It didn’t take much persuasion by Lachlan to make her agree, and he sensed that there was relief after her show of reluctance. The past few months had obviously been gruelling for her.

'So you've an auntie who's taken you in. What about a boyfriend?'

Lindsay blinked rapidly, trying to hold back sudden tears, and suddenly looked like the little girl she really was. 'He…he's in hospital. He had an accident.'

'Does he know about the baby?'

''Course he does.' She took a grubby tissue out of her sleeve and scrubbed her nose, sniffing. She twisted her hands together, screwing up the tissue and looked mournfully at Lachlan.

He smiled at her encouragingly. 'What's he done to himself—and which hospital is he in?'

'He fell from a roof and he's…he's really badly hurt.' She rubbed her eyes and whispered, 'We… we was living together. Then a week ago he was with a friend… He was trying to earn some money, and it happened. I only heard about it when Carl came and told me. I don't know how Greg is or anything… I think he's in that St Luke's Hospital.'

Something clicked inside Lachlan's head. He

frowned and leant forward. 'What did you say his name is, Lindsay?'

'Greg,' she whispered. 'Gregory Marsh. He said he knew a place he could get lead and stuff to sell—off someone he knew. He was doing it for me and the baby…' She gave a hiccuping sob. 'But he might be dead now, for all I know!'

Lachlan widened his eyes in surprise and smiled. 'Well, well, what a coincidence! I've good news for you. Greg isn't dead, although he's badly injured. I'm going to ask my colleague Dr Lennox to join us, because she may have more information about him. You see, we both happened to be there when your boyfriend had his accident.'

Lindsay stared in a dumbfounded way at Lachlan as if trying to work out what he meant. 'What d'you mean, you happened to be there?' she said falteringly.

'Because he had his accident just across the courtyard here, in the barn. Luckily we heard him fall and were able to help.'

Lachlan didn't go into detail, or mention the dodgy circumstances that surrounded Greg's accident—that was for another time. He lifted the internal phone and asked Christa if she could come in for a moment.

Lindsay shook her head. 'I don't understand. I thought he was going to a metal dealer's,' she mumbled. 'The thing is, I couldn't go back to the place we was living, not by myself. It was just a derelict building, so I went to my auntie's. At least she took me in. But when Greg comes out, he won't know where I've gone. He'll think I've scarpered.'

Lindsay looked at Lachlan piteously and he felt saddened by the car crash of a life that she was having. 'You never know,' he said comfortingly, 'we might be able to get a bed for you in the same hospital.'

Christa came into the room, eyebrows raised in enquiry. 'How can I help?' she asked.

She'd discarded her coat and was in a smart taupe-coloured suit with a slimline skirt and fitted jacket that emphasised the curves of her neat figure. Her auburn hair was drawn into a neat chignon to the back of her head and she looked cool, efficient and absolutely delectable.

Lachlan, unprepared for the jolt of his heart at her appearance, took a gulp of air. God, she was a knockout—he wasn't used to being distracted at work by any girl, however attractive, and it slightly baffled him. He liked to be in command of himself, in charge of the situation, like he had been in Australia. Plenty of pretty girls there, but none of them had seemed to have this unsettling effect that Christa was having on him.

He pulled himself together and said briskly, 'Ah, Dr Lennox. This is Lindsay Cooper—Lindsay, this is Dr Lennox. As I told you, she and I were at the scene when your boyfriend had his accident.' He turned to explain the position to Christa. 'I think that Lindsay needs bed rest and observation for a few days. Her BP's slightly up and she has definite signs of iron deficiency. Do you think there's any chance she could get a bed in St Luke's, where her boyfriend is?'

Christa smiled at the apprehensive girl. 'I'll do my best. Hello, Lindsay, so Greg's your boyfriend?'

Lindsay's voice cracked slightly. 'I want to see

him. I didn't know what had happened until Carl came and told me the next day…'

Poor kid—she looked totally exhausted and bleak, thought Christa compassionately.

'I can tell you that he's making good progress. He cracked one or two vertebrae in his back and his leg's broken, but luckily these are all things that can be mended, although they'll take some time.' She turned to Lachlan. 'I'll ring Mr Foster, the gynae consultant at St. Luke's, now and ask for Lindsay to be admitted.'

'Don't tell my parents where I am. Not that they care. They slung me out when they knew I was expecting anyway. They'll only make trouble for me and the baby.'

How could parents do that to their young daughter? wondered Christa almost in despair. Her eyes met Lachlan's in mutual sympathy for Lindsay, and he smiled down at the young girl and patted her shoulder reassuringly.

'We won't tell your parents if you don't want us to. But for the sake of your baby, you need help—you've done the hard part, coming in here. Now let the right people help you. I'll ask the practice nurse to help you onto the bed and then I can examine you.'

In a few minutes Sarah Duthey had helped Lindsay onto the bed and draped a towel over her lower abdomen to give an illusion of modesty. She stood by as Lachlan gently examined the high, firm mound of the girl's abdomen, and all the time he chatted to her, feeling the tension in her body gradually relax and watching her clenched fists slacken.

'Now I'm just trying to find out roughly how far on your pregnancy is,' he said soothingly. 'At the moment the baby feels fine, but Nurse here will take some blood from you so that we can run a few tests to see how well *you* are. Do you know what you want—a boy or a girl?'

A glimmer of a smile appeared on Lindsay's lips. 'Don't care, so long as it's not a garden gnome!'

The two doctors and Sarah laughed. Lindsay was beginning to trust them, and that had been achieved, thought Christa shrewdly, because Lachlan Maguire was pretty good with vulnerable, edgy people. Not everyone would have been able to get through the hedgehog prickliness that Lindsey used against the world.

'I think from your size, Lindsay, that you're probably seven or eight months pregnant—that means we've got enough time to improve your iron levels and feed you up before the baby comes,' said Lachlan.

Lindsay propped herself up. 'So what do I have to do now?' she asked.

'We'll get an ambulance to take you to the hospital, where you'll be able to put your feet up.'

Sarah tucked a sheet over her. 'How about a nice cup of tea, love, while you're waiting?' she said.

Lindsay smiled and nodded, then lay back on the bed and closed her eyes, looking as if she could drift off to sleep there and then.

'The poor wee lamb,' murmured Sarah as she passed Lachlan and Christa. 'All she needs is some TLC.'

Later, when most of the staff were having coffee after morning surgery in the little kitchen, Christa said to Lachlan, 'You did well to get

Lindsay to agree to go to hospital. I never thought she'd go.'

He grinned and shook his head. 'I think she was secretly glad to be taken care of. She'd obviously been living rough at some point. But Mother Nature's curious—you can get a girl who takes tremendous care of herself, eats all the right things, doesn't smoke or drink and she can end up with all kind of problems. And here we've got young Lindsay, undernourished and in general poor health, and her baby seems to be developing normally and a good size.'

'Fancy Greg Marsh being her boyfriend. God, one trembles a bit for her, relying on him to help her.'

'I think she's pretty clued up—she had the good sense to go to her aunt's when Greg didn't come back to her after the accident. She's probably going to be the one looking after Greg!'

Alice Smith came in with a pile of files and said cheerily, 'You're getting a pretty good press, Lachlan. This morning several of the patients asked me if you were the hero who saved the day and moved a dangerous beam when that boy was injured. I think your surgeries are going to be booked up for months ahead! And I've had the local paper on the phone, wanting a photo of you both for their "People of the Month" slot—they're coming some time today to get it into this week's edition.'

It wasn't surprising that patients took to Lachlan, reflected Christa. That special blend of kindliness and authority that she'd seen him display with Lindsay reminded her poignantly of another medic she'd worked with, and that was Isobel Maguire, Lachlan's mother—the best-loved doctor in the district.

The next few days were busy but very satisfactory in that Lachlan seemed to gel into the practice well and Christa began to relax. They had no verbal spats, and the subject of the development didn't come up. The only worry was the supposedly delicious meal she was going to provide for Ahmed Kumar, the director of information technology, and Lachlan on the Thursday evening. Eventually she'd decided on some venison in red wine and juniper berries, in her slow-cook oven.

Janet, her next-door neighbour, who always took Titan for a long walk in the middle of the day, would switch it on and by the time Christa got home it would be ready! She imagined Lachlan's gratified and impressed smile when he took the first mouthful—hopefully so much more delicious than the ready meals he'd been microwaving!

She was surprised when she arrived home that evening to find that no tantalising smell greeted her as she went into the kitchen—just Titan galloping across the floor to give her his usual extravagant welcome. She lifted the lid of the casserole and dipped a spoon in to sample the gravy and the meat—stone cold! What had gone wrong with the blessed thing? Then she noticed with increasing horror that the light was out on the cooker. Janet must have forgotten to do it—or, more probably, Christa had forgotten to tell her!

'Marvellous!' she muttered, slamming the lid

back on the casserole. 'What on earth shall I do now? They'll be here in half an hour!'

She peered hopefully into the fridge. Nothing much in it except for eggs, a few shrivelled little mushrooms and two tomatoes. Not enough for the banquet Lachlan must be expecting. She was pondering whether she had time to rush to the supermarket when the telephone rang. It was Ahmed on the line, sounding very weary and fed up.

'So sorry, Christa, I'm still at Heathrow. I was in London for a meeting and the flight's been cancelled. Can you believe it? I probably won't be home till tomorrow now.'

Of course she could believe it, thought Christa wryly—it was that kind of an evening! Any minute now Lachlan would call to say he couldn't come either, which of course would solve the dilemma she had of nothing to produce in the way of food! She commiserated with Ahmed and assured him that it didn't matter, then flopped down in a chair as she considered what to do.

Maybe, she thought hesitantly, she should ring Lachlan and say the evening was all off for now, and they'd arrange it for another time. A funny little feeling of disappointment niggled at the back of her mind—despite the fact that Lachlan coming to be fed that evening had worried her all day.

She brought up his number on her phone, but the only response she got was for the caller to leave a message and he would get back to her as soon as possible. He was probably on his way already, she thought in a sudden panic. She just hoped he liked omelettes!

Christa flicked a look at her watch—just time for a quick shower and a change of clothes. If she couldn't produce a good meal at least she could try and look fresh and less work-weary. She scrambled into a pair of jeans and a loose-fitting blue silk blouse, gave her hair a quick brush and her lips a quick slick of gloss just before the doorbell rang. Funny how her heart started hammering against her chest. After all, this wasn't a date. It was just an evening together to discuss practice affairs—nothing exciting at all. Titan bounded joyfully to the door. He liked visitors, and barked a welcome.

Christa gulped nervously and murmured to Titan, 'I should have put him off, shouldn't I?'

But, then, she said sternly to herself, this was purely a polite social evening for two new colleagues to get to know each other, and just because Ahmed couldn't come there was no reason why she and Lachlan shouldn't spend the evening together.

And then she opened the door and swallowed hard as she looked at Lachlan. She *had* done the right thing after all! The porch light threw a sort of halo around him, investing him with a bright glamour. Like her, he had changed into jeans, as well as a loose cream sweater over an open-necked shirt. Casual suited him so much—he looked younger, more relaxed, and that Australian tan made his eyes seem bluer, his teeth whiter. She took a deep breath. She had to put his good looks to the back of her mind because, of course, she had told him friendship was the only thing on the cards—nothing else. Madness to think otherwise!

She brushed a tendril of hair back from her forehead, hoping she looked more composed than she felt, and said unnecessarily, 'Oh, there you are!'

He stood there, smiling engagingly, with a bottle of wine in one hand and a large box of chocolates in the other, his eyes lingering for a microsecond over her tall, slender figure.

'Hello, there, Dr Lennox! I've been dreaming of this meal all day. All through Mrs Phillip's description of the trouble she's been having with her haemorrhoids, and likewise Mr Burn's saga about his bad feet, my stomach's been rumbling with anticipation…'

Christa pulled a wry face. 'Oh, God. I'm awfully sorry, but I'm afraid your dreams of a meal are going to be dashed,' she said, leading him through to the little living room. 'Dinner's off, and I hope you're not allergic to eggs!'

CHAPTER SIX

LACHLAN THREW BACK his head and laughed. 'That's a great welcome! But an omelette would be fine—anything that doesn't come in a fast-food packet!'

'The thing is,' Christa explained, 'I forgot to tell my lovely neighbour to turn on the slow cooker, and then Ahmed rang to say he's stuck at Heathrow. The evening's been a disaster before it's even started!'

'Oh, I don't know,' said Lachlan, his eyes twinkling at her. 'I think we can manage without Ahmed or the full-blown meal. Tell you what—I'll uncork this wine and you start throwing the eggs in the pan. How about that?'

And that is what she did, and after a mushroom and tomato omelette and a bit of salad, along with two glasses of very nice Sauvignon

Blanc, somehow the evening didn't seem such a disaster after all.

There wasn't a dearth of conversation—Lachlan had plenty of questions to ask about the practice, and although they talked about improvements to the surgery, the vexed question of the development of the land never came up.

The dining table was in an alcove in the little sitting room, and a wood fire burned in the grate—it all looked cosy and warm. Christa had decorated the walls in a soft cream and the sofa and chairs were covered in modern striped upholstery. Lachlan looked around approvingly, taking in the neat pine dresser against the wall and the little desk under the window—just the right size for the room.

'This is a lovely little place,' he said. 'You seem to have struck just the right note. Not too old-fashioned, and it looks bright and fresh. I'm at a complete loss to know what to do with Ardenleigh. The rooms are beautiful, but I've not a clue how to furnish them. I'd like a fresh start, I think.'

The wine seemed to have loosened Christa's

tongue and she found herself saying brightly, 'Could I help at all? I rather enjoy planning the colours in rooms'

He pounced on the idea enthusiastically. 'That would be fantastic! Let's make a firm date for you to come and look at it all. The place is really far too big. I'm beginning to realise that, and yet, well, it's such a beautiful house, and although there's just me, it's always been a dream of mine to live in it again.'

'Your mother wanted you to have it, didn't she? She left it to you. And as for it being too big, you're bound to have a family eventually.'

Lachlan raised an amused eyebrow. 'Am I? I don't think I'm the type to marry, settle down and have children. At least, I've no plans in that direction. Keep your options open, I say!'

So just like Colin, then, play the field, never give yourself completely, thought Christa grimly. Love and commitment didn't seem to be in their vocabularies.

Lachlan watched her expression and said quietly, as if in explanation, 'Marriages that break down can have a devastating effect on a family—I know that. Never give promises you may not be able to keep.'

Christa bit her lip. He was probably referring to his own parents' marriage, and it certainly seemed to have affected him deeply, to the point of him leaving his home. Her own father had died some years ago, but he and her mother had had a very happy and loving marriage. Christa's childhood had been idyllic, and although it had been horrible when her father had died, her mother had borne her sadness with stoicism and had taken up new interests and made plenty of friends.

Lachlan rose from his chair and walked over to the fire, standing with his back to it.

'Talking of families—what about you? I can't believe that there hasn't been someone special in your life.'

He was bound to find out sooner or later, because Colin dumping her for someone else wasn't a secret. That was part of the heartbreak, it being so public. Everyone in Errin Bridge had known they were an item. And then everyone had begun to realise that he had been playing the field at the same time as dating her—everyone except her, of course, cocooned in her safe little world of romance and love.

'There was someone once, not any more.' Christa's voice sounded casual—too casual, as if she was making a deliberate effort to make a broken love affair sound of no consequence. Lachlan's blue eyes looked at her astutely.

'You had a bad experience, then?'

'Like loads of people, it didn't work out. End of story,' she said flatly.

'It's never the end completely, though, is it?' murmured Lachlan. 'Hard to switch off from loving someone with all your heart to feeling nothing at all for them.'

'Very perceptive of you.' She shrugged. 'I learned something from the experience, and I realise now that Colin and I wouldn't have been right for each other anyway.'

Lachlan frowned. 'Colin…?'

Christa shrugged. 'Colin Maitland—the one you used to go fishing with when you were a little boy. He worked at the practice for a while.' She added flippantly, 'He did a pretty good impression of a rat while I was going out with him.'

'He's always had a reputation,' growled Lachlan. 'Now, there's a man I thought would never settle down to marriage. You told me he was married now, didn't you?'

'Oh, yes.' Christa gave a mirthless laugh. 'He found her while he was going out with me—the word's "two-timing", I think.' She rose from the sofa and went over to Lachlan and picked up the photo on the desk. 'This was him on his wedding day.'

Lachlan took the photo from her and looked at it, then said slowly, 'Why did he marry this girl if he liked to "play the field", as you said?'

'Because Paula became pregnant, and she's the daughter of the MP for this area. As a local doctor Colin's name would have been mud if he'd abandoned her. But it was a shock, I can tell you, when I heard about the engagement from someone else—not from Colin!'

'What a sod. How long had you gone out with him?'

'About two years. I was mad about him—and I thought he loved me too.'

The words hung in the air, bleak and heartbreaking, revealing only too well the story of shattered dreams. Christa gave a shaky little laugh. 'I'll never be so naïve again!'

'Did you go to the wedding?' he asked softly.

'No. That was something I couldn't bring myself to do. So he sent me that photo.'

'As if to show you what you'd missed out on? What a bastard!' He frowned. 'Why on earth do you keep a photo up of the man on his wedding day?'

Christa looked at the floor, twisting her hands together, and whispered after a short silence, 'Because...because I needed to remind myself every day that he wasn't worth crying about... but it didn't seem to work...'

Something in the catch of Christa's voice made Lachlan look closely at her. She had bowed her head, but he could see a tear rolling slowly down the curve of her cheek, and then she put up a hand and brushed it away impatiently. In an instant his arm was round her shoulders, hugging her to his body and wiping away her tears with a handkerchief.

'Christa—sweetheart. I'm sorry, I didn't mean

to hurt you, to stir up old memories. What a dolt I am!' He rocked her backwards and forwards as one would to comfort a child, stroking her hair gently. 'He's always been a selfish sod, out for his own pleasure, never mind who he tramples over. Perhaps that's why we lost touch.'

'It's not your fault I'm upset,' snuffled Christa, blowing her nose and shaking her head. 'I'm an idiot to cry over the man. The thing is, the week before he married Paula he came round and begged me to go back to him.'

'But he was engaged to someone else. How the hell could he do that?' Lachlan looked down at her, and a flicker of amused sympathy flickered in his eyes. 'Is that the reason I overheard you say you wouldn't get married for a million pounds?'

A wry smile touched Christa's lips. 'Can you blame me?'

'Of course I don't. And since then there's been no one?'

She shook her head and looked up at him with some spirit. 'Absolutely not! I can do without men and sex for quite a few years, thank you very much—too much hassle!'

He chuckled and looked down at her with dancing eyes. 'That's my feisty girl,' he murmured, giving her a comforting squeeze. 'But I wouldn't put a time limit on your celibate life, it's a hell of a long time to be lonely.'

She laughed back at him, with a sudden feeling of release in having told her sad little story. Lachlan was right, she couldn't condemn herself to singledom for years just because a man had hurt her in the past. She relaxed against him, and his arm around her felt comfortable, safe.

'Perhaps you're right…' she murmured. 'Maybe I should live a bit, play the field. Enjoy life!'

He stroked her soft cheek. 'You can't live in the past, Christa, or let the darned man ruin your future.'

In the background the wood fire crackled and Titan snored slightly in his basket. The atmosphere was warm and intimate, just the two of them together. They smiled at each other, then gradually something changed between them and the smiles faded. They were so close—standing hip to hip, her soft breasts pressed against his body, his face so near hers she could see the little grey streaks in his hair, smell the male smell of him, the clean, soapy freshness of his body.

Of course it wasn't the first time Christa had felt that dangerous thrill of attraction towards Lachlan Maguire—she'd tried to suppress it then, but now it was like a red-hot flame flickering treacherously through her body, unstoppable. And as he held her close with his arm around her, she was only too aware of how much he wanted her as well. She knew exactly what was going to happen—could see the dark need that mirrored hers in his eyes.

Was she crazy to blank out the loneliness of the past two years by making love to a man she knew wasn't in the market for any emotional attachment, someone she'd known for a bare two weeks, for heaven's sake? But, then, she was under no illusions about Lachlan Maguire. He'd told her he didn't believe in lasting love. She was going into this with her eyes open. And, hey, she wasn't into commitment any more either, was she? She just wanted to be desired, to have fun once more.

He was still stroking her cheek gently and she put her head against his chest. 'Lachlan…' she faltered. 'It's been so long. I think I've almost forgotten how to…'

'Oh, no, you haven't, sweetheart,' he said huskily, and lifting her face to his he brought his mouth down on her full, tremulous lips, kissing them softly at first and then more demandingly.

And whether it was the uninhibiting influence of the wine, or because she had just unburdened herself to him, Christa threw caution and sense to the winds, and it felt natural and right that she should wind her arms around his neck, arching her body against him in instant response, opening her mouth languidly to his. Her insides liquefied with longing, her heart beating a mad tattoo in her chest. Two lonely people and no strings attached, fulfilling a mutual need. Wasn't that what she wanted? The bitter memory of Colin's betrayal faded into the background.

Lachlan gazed down at her in the half-light of the room, examining her face—the black lashes fringing those wide, amber eyes, her full, soft lips and the tendrils of hair across her forehead.

'Christa,' he whispered raggedly, 'you are so bloody delectable. When I came back, I didn't expect to find someone like you around.' He wrapped his arms around her tightly and put his forehead to hers. 'You do know where this could lead, don't you? Do you really want this to happen? Will you be sorry later?'

And she almost laughed because surely it was too late to have second thoughts with his hard frame clamped around hers and every erogenous zone in her body demanding release that very moment. She felt as if she were on a wave of euphoria, light-hearted, free of the sad thoughts that had plagued her when she'd thought of Colin.

'Of course I want it to happen. I want it very much.' She held back from him for a moment, her eyes dancing. 'Is this what you meant by being "friendly colleagues"?'

His face split into a grin. 'Certainly—if you want to interpret it like that,' he murmured.

Lachlan pulled her gently down onto the

sheepskin rug on the floor and unbuttoned the silk blouse and the wispy bra she was wearing. Then he tore off his shirt, and his hard and demanding body was on her soft skin, his lips trailing down to the little hollow in her neck, his skilful hands exploring her most secret places, arousing her to fever pitch.

And suddenly Christa realised she hadn't forgotten what it was like to make love, and somehow it was more marvellous than she ever remembered. She ignored the tiny seed of doubt that hovered at the back of her mind—could she really live for the day, keep her feelings for Lachlan as casual as he wanted to, after what was happening?

Afterwards they lay curled around each other, and Christa fell asleep in Lachlan's arms. He watched the embers of the fire flickering and their shadows on the wall, and the most incredible feeling of happiness swept through him. He looked down at her face against his chest. God, she was beautiful—her skin as soft as a peach and those large expressive eyes that were a running commentary on her feelings.

He'd certainly never led a celibate life—plenty of girls had given him every encouragement, but no one had awoken in him this strange and sudden tenderness he felt for Christa, or moved him like she had. Dammit, this wasn't supposed to happen, was it? This was meant to be a lighthearted romp, neither of them committing to the other…pure lust on either side. And yet it didn't seem to be working like that for him at all. What should have been a one-off, ships-that-passed-in-the-night scenario felt like just the beginning, the start of something precious and exciting.

Only a day or two ago he'd vowed that Christa was the last person he should become involved with—not just because of their families' entwined histories but because he wasn't going to be ruled by his mother's wishes and ever ask Christa to marry him. And he still believed that, didn't he? Then he thought of the photos he'd found in his mother's desk and their poignant words on the back: *My darling son.*

An ache for something once cherished and

lost for ever overcame him. Perhaps after all his mother had only wanted the best for him—and yet he still shied away from that complete commitment to another person, was still sceptical of the 'Till death do us part' bit. He'd seen how breaking vows could lead to broken lives.

Christa stirred in his arms and opened her eyes, looking into his, and smiled sleepily.

'Hello,' she murmured. 'That was…wonderful, wasn't it?'

He held her close to him and kissed her tousled hair. 'Yes,' he whispered. 'Quite wonderful.'

It was late, very late, when Lachlan left. Christa walked slowly through the living room into her bedroom, her heart dancing with a happy excitement she hadn't felt for a very long time. She saw the photo of Colin on his wedding day, and picked it up, looking at it scornfully.

'I don't need the memory of you any more, Colin Maitland,' she said calmly. 'I've my own life to lead now, without your shadow hanging over me.'

She dropped it in the waste-paper basket and went to bed. Christa enjoyed the best sleep she'd had for many weeks.

Alfie Jackson sat bellowing loudly on his grandmother's knee in front of Christa. His eyes were round and frightened behind wire-rimmed spectacles and his mouth a large wide 'O'. He was three years old and dressed in a policeman's uniform, the helmet sitting crookedly on his head. He looked utterly adorable, and completely inconsolable, holding one hand tightly in the other.

'So what happened, Mrs Pye?' asked Christa loudly above the noise.

Mrs Pye, plump and flustered, said helplessly, 'I feel so guilty. I'm supposed to be looking after the little lad today—my daughter's got this interview for a part-time job this afternoon. I was getting Alfie ready for a party and he opened a cupboard to get something out and then slammed it on his finger! It looks so sore and I don't know what I can do…'

Alfie turned and buried his face in his grandmother's ample bosom, sobs shaking his little body. In between the sobs could be heard the words 'Not my fault…the door hurt me!'

'Of course it's not your fault, Alfie!' soothed Christa. She came round the desk and bent down beside him. 'Won't you just let me have a little peep at this poorly finger, sweetheart?'

Predictably, more screams and Christa sighed inwardly. It had been quite a gruelling day, including a quick dash over to see the old shepherd, Fred Logan, who'd developed a urinary infection and had been taken to hospital. He'd needed a lot of persuasion to do that! Dealing with a frightened child in great pain was going to be even more difficult. She pulled open a desk drawer and pulled out a small toy car, wound it up and placed it on the floor, where it proceeded to flicker and whirr, with lights flashing on and off as it whizzed round the room.

'Look at that, Alfie—look!' cried Christa, above the child's sobs.

A very quick peep from his grandmother's bosom, and then a more prolonged stare as the toy banged into the wall, somersaulted and started off again. In those few seconds Christa managed to prise Alfie's hands apart and saw for herself the little boy's blackened nail and swollen finger, incongruous on that small, chubby hand.

She winced. 'That is one sore little finger,' she said to Mrs Pye.

'I suppose it'll have to be drilled, won't it, Doctor? Oh, dear, I don't think I could bear to watch...'

'I can do something much more quickly and more accurately than that,' Christa assured her. She lifted the internal phone and pressed the button for Lachlan's room. 'Have you got a minute? And a match or a lighter?'

In the few seconds it took for Lachlan to appear Christa had taken a needle out of a packet and a pair of tweezers from a box in her drawer. Mrs Pye looked nervously at her.

'Wouldn't it be better to take Alfie to hospital and give him an anaesthetic?'

'If we can release the pressure now, before the blood begins to clot, it will be instant relief. By the time you get to hospital it would be too late to do much,' explained Christa.

Lachlan came into the room, his imposing figure somehow reassuring, his eyes taking in the scene at a glance then coming to rest on Christa. Their gazes locked for a heart-stopping moment, but even in that moment she could read the messages of desire and need in his eyes, the memory of Lachlan's body moulded to hers, his hands caressing her, bringing her to fever pitch coming back to her in graphic detail… What a difference a night had made! A rush of adrenalin flickered through her, made her pulse start to race.

She was brought back down to earth as Lachlan turned to Mrs Pye and Alfie, and said briskly, "I thought I could hear a young man in pain over the intercom. What's happened?'

Christa pulled herself together, almost ashamed that she'd allowed thoughts of their lovemaking to intrude on her professional life.

'Alfie's got a subungual haematoma on his finger,' explained Christa succinctly.

Lachlan winced. 'Ooh, poor little chap, that's very nasty. But, as Dr Lennox has no doubt told you, we'll soon have him right as rain again. Here's the matches. I pinched them from the kitchen.'

'Now, Mrs Pye, I want you to hold Alfie very firmly,' instructed Christa. 'I'll hold his hand and if we keep it steady, it'll take literally a few moments.'

Mrs Pye gave a faint squawk of horror. 'I hope I don't faint,' she quavered, her eyes on stalks as she watched Christa strike a match and Lachlan hold the pin with the tweezers in the flame until the tip of the pin glowed red.

Alfie redoubled his screams, but Christa held his hand in a vice-like grip while Lachlan pressed the red-hot pin firmly onto the blackened fingernail. There was a slight hiss and a faint trace of smoke as the pin burnt through the nail and a tiny globule of blood appeared through the hole.

Christa bound the small finger with a gauze strip. 'I can guarantee that it's hardly hurting at all now. Am I right, young man?'

A few residual sobs from Alfie, and then he looked down at his covered finger. 'Is it better now?' he asked.

'It will heal very quickly. You can even go to your party now if you want to!'

'Well, I'm blessed!' murmured Mrs Pye in awestruck tones. 'Can you credit it, just a pin and a match!'

Christa smiled. 'We aim to please—but don't try it at home.'

Mrs Pye shuddered. 'Certainly not!'

The little boy slid off his grandmother's knee, his policeman's helmet at a rakish angle over his brow, and Lachlan crouched down beside him.

'You've been a very brave policeman,' he said. 'It so happens we give medals for brave policemen, don't we, Dr Lennox? You're a hero, Alfie!'

He reached into his jacket pocket and pulled out a metal badge with 'Bravery Award' imprinted on the front and stuck it on Alfie's little jacket. Alfie looked down at it and then a beam split his round face.

'Am I?' he said, looking at Lachlan round-eyed, and then turned to his grandmother. 'I'm a hero, Grandma!'

Lachlan ruffled the little boy's hair and smiled. 'Enjoy your party.'

Mrs Pye smiled tremulously at the two doctors. 'Oh, thank you so much, I'm really grateful. Come on, Alfie, love.'

She took the little boy's hand and they walked out, an incongruous couple—the large elderly lady and a very small policeman, now chattering happily to his grandmother.

'A very different child from the one who came in,' observed Christa. 'You've made a friend of that young man!'

Lachlan smiled. 'It was a job well done,' he commented. 'They call it "trephining", don't they? A neat little trick!'

'Did it on a short course called "Surgery on a Shoestring".' She grinned.

'Very droll…' He caught her arm as she went past him to the desk and swung her towards him. 'Christa…about last night…'

She gazed at him innocently, but a smile quivered at the corners of her mouth. 'What about last night?'

He grinned and ran his finger down her cheek. 'Don't be a minx…and why do you look so unutterably gorgeous? You should look exhausted after what we did last night…'

'I slept rather well,' Christa said demurely.

'Well, among other exciting things, last night you said you'd help me with ideas for the house—don't forget about it! Perhaps you could come over one Saturday or Sunday and we could have a walk and eat a pub lunch after you've had a look at things?'

It sounded idyllic—so unlike the weekends over the past months, which, although there had been many fun times with friends, playing tennis or riding in the hills, had been without that thrilling excitement of being with someone who was the sexiest thing on two legs!

'I might be able to manage that,' Christa said gravely. 'I'll pop round with some sample pots of colour from the decorator's shop in the village.'

Lachlan's hand went behind her neck and he drew her to him, kissing her full on the lips. 'I look forward to it very much indeed...' He held her away from him, and his eyes twinkled at her. 'Don't let it be too long!' Then he left the room.

Christa hoped her flushed cheeks had faded and that Alice didn't notice anything untoward in her appearance when she came in a few minutes later with the post.

And then the phone rang, and it was the community nurse, Lorna, to say that Bessie Logan, alone in the cottage, had fallen after Fred had been taken to hospital, and although she was uninjured was finding it difficult to stand unsupported.

'Bessie managed to ring her son, Ian, in Inverness, and he got hold of the rapid response team from the hospital, who came and got her up,' explained Lorna. 'She's adamant she won't go to hospital because she thinks Fred will be back soon and she must be there for him.'

'I'll come immediately,' promised Christa. 'Surgery's nearly over and Lachlan can cover for me.'

On her way through the hills, back to the Logans' for the second time that day, Christa started singing, filled with a joy of life that she hadn't had for so long. She'd always loved her job—the variety of it, helping people through the highs and lows of their lives—but the sadness of Colin's betrayal of her had tarnished that pleasure. How strange that a man she'd been determined to dislike should have changed her whole perception of life in a few hours!

She considered the Logans and the support they were going to need. Christa didn't doubt that Bessie would not be at all eager to go into a retirement home, and immediate plans for her future would have to be discussed very tactfully when she arrived at Bessie's.

Bessie was sitting up in bed, sipping a cup of tea and chatting with Lorna and three members of the rapid response team. Ian, her son, had also arrived, looking big and brawny in the small room, his face creased with worry.

'Good to see you, Doctor,' he said. 'Mum and Dad have given us a bit of a fright today, what with Mum's fall and Dad being taken in to hospital.'

Bessie looked frail and frightened. 'I'm sure they're going to send me to a home, but I don't want to go, really I don't,' she said in a faint voice, her faded blue eyes looking pleadingly at Christa. 'I'll be all right. I just took a tumble, but I'll be fine.'

She looked anxiously from Christa to the team and Christa went up and took her thin little hand, lying on the counterpane.

'Don't worry,' Christa said reassuringly. 'We'll sort something out, Bessie. Nobody's going to send you anywhere—only if you need nursing for a little while. How is your walking?'

'I'm not too bad with a frame.' Bessie sounded rather defiant, as if to tell them all that she could manage very well.

'We think maybe she's not been eating, with worry about Fred, and that could be why she's a little weak,' explained Lorna.

'I think we'll take some blood for anaemia and thyroid function,' said Christa.

Ian stood by, twisting his cap in his hands and looking frustrated. 'I'm concerned,' he said in a low voice to Christa. 'Mum being all alone in the hills here—it's not satisfactory. I'd really like her to come home with me.' He directed his words to his mother. 'It would just be for a few days, Mum.'

'But I need to be here for your father. He could come home any day.'

'I don't think he'll be back for a week at least,' said Lorna. 'It's going to take a bit of time to get on top of the infection he's got. Would you not go back with Ian for a little while?'

Bessie tried again. 'What about one of those disc things that you wear round your neck and can call someone if you fall?'

'You're still a long way away in the middle of the night, Mum. Please, you know I'll worry so much if you're by yourself.' He turned to the others in the room. 'I'd come and stay here but I'm in the middle of a new job—I don't think it would go down well if I took time off.'

Bessie sighed. 'Well, perhaps for just a few days, then. Just to get my strength back.' She looked dolefully at Christa. 'That Shona of his—she's a bully, though!'

They all laughed, and Ian threw his eyes to the ceiling. 'You need looking after, Mum. You've been working so hard here, and a bit of care and feeding up is what you need, and Shona's looking forward to doing that!'

'Well, when you come back we'll put forward

a plan for your needs,' said Christa. 'Hopefully Fred will be back then.'

Ian came out with Christa to the car. 'It's been difficult, Doctor,' he said wearily. 'I know she's a wonderful old lady, but she can be as stubborn as an ox! I really think my parents would be much safer in a retirement home.'

'No one wants to leave their own home, Ian—we can't force her. We'll assess their needs for long-term care when she's come back here. Who knows, in the end she may see for herself that life is going to be very difficult looking after Fred and herself out here. Why don't you and Shona start looking around homes to see what they're like? Just groundwork really.'

He nodded. 'Aye, we'll do that. Anyway, I'll bring her home with me now and I'll be in contact with you regarding Dad and his progress.'

It was practically dark by the time Christa returned home. She parked the car and as she fumbled for the key in her bag, the door opened in the next house and her neighbour, Janet, came out, with a bowl of flowers in her hands.

'Hi, Christa, I saw these on your doorstep when I came back from taking Titan for a walk. I took them in, in case that cat down the road started playing with them. Aren't they lovely?'

Christa took them from her and buried her nose in the delicate arrangement of tiny tête-à-tête daffodils and freesias in a small blue pottery bowl.

'Mmm, they smell so fresh and springlike,' she said.

'Looks like you've got an admirer,' teased Janet.

Christa tore open the note that was stuck on the side. It said, 'Thank you for the most delicious omelette I've ever had in my life.'

She giggled, then grinned at Janet and stuffed the note in her pocket. 'Only a thank-you note for a pretty awful meal I made for the new partner in the practice,' she said lightly.

And although she glowed with pleasure as she put the little arrangement on the table, she told herself sternly that it was just a polite but amusing gesture of thanks, and that the evening had meant nothing more to Lachlan than a bit of fun between two people who were free agents.

Of course they were attracted to each other, but hadn't they agreed, as adults who knew their own minds, to keep it cool without commitment? She smiled wryly to herself. Deep down, didn't she yearn for more than that with Lachlan? Something that would involve a meaningful future?

CHAPTER SEVEN

Please be ready at seven-thirty tonight for a brainstorm meeting re work, etc., to expand on what we did the other evening. We need to discuss that thoroughly. We'll go to local restaurant. Lachlan.

CHRISTA GIGGLED. READING her e-mails at work was usually pretty routine, but this one gave her a jolt of delight. She wondered just how much work would be discussed at the 'brainstorm meeting'! The 'etc.' bit gave her a clue that there would be more to it than talk about the practice, and a lovely feeling of anticipation at meeting him later on kept shooting through her all day.

This was her first 'proper' date with Lachlan Maguire, but she was determined to take things slowly, stick to her airy intentions of keeping everything casual and emotionally detached between them. Well, she could try, anyway!

She sent him a reply. 'Look forward to discussing programme...'

Christa was ready hours before seven-thirty. It seemed like a family of butterflies was fluttering in her stomach, and as if this first proper invitation from Lachlan to go out with him was one of the most important dates she'd ever had in her life. She'd gone through every outfit in her wardrobe and discarded them all as unsuitable. During the past year, shopping for clothes had not featured much in her life. Finally she'd selected a pair of black trousers with a soft blue angora jumper that was warm without being suffocating.

She looked doubtfully at herself in the mirror as she brushed her hair. Was she looking too casual? Not casual enough? Then she laughed, wondering just why she was getting in such a spin. It was just going to be a normal, pleasant evening of chat, wasn't it? But it had been a long time since she felt this sort of excitement before a date. Had she really felt this pent up before going out with Colin? She bit her lip, remembering how she had sent caution to the winds and had had a wild affair with him that had all ended in tears.

She certainly wasn't going to be like that with Lachlan—however much she longed to. He wasn't for commitment and if anyone got hurt it would be her. If she'd learned anything from her past mistakes it was to be careful when it came to love. Just because she and Lachlan had had an unexpected fling one night, it didn't mean that was on the agenda for every date!

She peeped out of the window—the snow had started falling heavily and she suspected the wind would be as sharp as a honed knife. When it was cold in Errin Bridge it was really cold. She put on a coat her mother had given her, a long cream suede with a sheepskin lining, and plonked a Cossack hat made of fake fur on her head, then went to the door when she heard the bell.

Lachlan had on a large quilted jacket and fleecy hat with ear flaps, his clothes covered with a dusting of snow. He ran his gaze slowly over Christa, taking in the way the tendrils of her auburn hair curled round the white hat, the contrast of her flushed cheeks against the cream of the coat.

'Wow,' he said softly. 'You look like a snow queen…'

He leant forward and brushed her mouth with his lips, his cheek cold against hers. Christa felt herself go limp with desire—so much for keeping things light and casual! If he'd suggested giving up on the meal and going inside to make love, her good intentions might have floated out of the window.

'How gorgeous are you?' he whispered, drawing back and looking down at her with those sexy eyes of his.

'Well, you look as if you've just landed at an airport!' She grinned. 'Very macho and rugged.'

He grimaced. 'Thank you! Good job I kept this old hat—I used to use it when I was in the Flying Doctor service. It's come in useful for this weather, although I don't think it matches up to your outfit in any way. By the way, I hope you're hungry!'

Anticipation seemed to have taken away Christa's appetite. She'd been longing for this all day, and now the time was here she couldn't think of a thing she wanted to eat!

'Matelli's' restaurant was small and intimate and quite busy. There were red and white tablecloths gaily covering the candlelit tables, and on every wall were murals of sunny Italian scenes from the Bay of Naples to hilly views of Tuscany. In a corner a young man was playing Neapolitan songs softly on a guitar, and Christa felt that it was like stepping into another country after the wintry conditions outside.

Paolo Matelli, the owner, made a fuss of them as he led them to a table in an alcove, talking in a strong Italian accent.

'Ah! My favourite doctors! My bad back ees completely better, thanks to you, Dr Maguire! I miss your dear mother very much—but you are taking over very well! And, Dr Lennox, you look after my wife so well when she had her last baby! Look! I show you how well the bambino does!'

He whipped out a little leather folder and opened it, revealing several photos of a bouncing baby boy. Then, as the two doctors admired the photos, he fussed around, putting napkins in front of them with a flourish, pouring water into glasses.

'He's beautiful, Paolo. What do you call him?' said Christa.

'Vincente. He's very good, the best baby in the world!' Paolo's eyes twinkled at them. 'I tell you, there is nothing like a happy family to keep you going, eh? I trust that, like me, you will be blessed too!'

'I hope I will, Paolo,' said Lachlan quietly. 'And you're right—everyone needs a happy family.'

Christa looked at him compassionately. You didn't have to scratch very much beneath the surface for the experiences in Lachlan's own family to be recalled in the flicker of sadness in his blue eyes, and a shadow passing over his face.

Paolo put menus before them. 'Well, take my

advice, and don't leave it too late. You have to be young to cope with five of them!'

'Five children?' remarked Lachlan, his grave face breaking into a grin. 'I'd like children but I think five of them might test me a little.'

A little throb of longing lodged somewhere in Christa's brain, the wistful thought that she would love to have his babies—any amount! She looked at his face as he gravely studied the menu. She'd seen him dealing with youngsters over the past few weeks and had thought what a great dad he'd make. Perhaps he'd be strict, but fun and loving, learning from what had happened in his own life.

For goodness' sake, what are you like, Christa? she thought wryly. You're only on a first proper date with the man and already you're making him a father!

Lachlan looked at Christa across the table. The light in the restaurant was muted, but in the glow of the candlelight her auburn hair looked lustrous and her eyes as warm as a summer's day. When she looked down, her thick eyelashes shadowed her peachy cheeks. God, she was perfect! He longed to kiss her full mouth, to run his hands over the light blue angora jumper she was wearing, feel the softness of her breasts underneath. The sudden heat of desire rushed through him—for the first time in his life he knew that he wanted more from a girl than a light-hearted liaison, but he didn't want to rush things. Christa had had her heart broken before, she probably wasn't ready for commitment yet! Paolo came up to him, holding a bottle of champagne.

'I hope you accept this from our family—just to help make the evening a happy one!' He popped the cork and poured the sparkling liquid into two fluted glasses. He beamed benignly at them both. 'There! You celebrate, yes?'

'Thank you, Paolo—we'll do our best! We've a lot to discuss.' Lachlan's eyes held Christa's, something very tender in their warm depths, and she felt her heart turn over with happiness.

She laughed as they chinked their glasses together. 'I thought you wanted to have a "brainstorm meeting" to discuss work,' she said impishly.

'First things first—let's order some food. I'm

starving! I believe Paolo's the best cook in the north east of Scotland.'

'I know what I'm having—scallops in wine sauce.'

'Make that two,' said Lachlan. 'And I think this bottle of champagne will go down well with that.'

Paolo bustled away and Lachlan picked up his glass. 'To us, sweetheart…' His blue eyes were warm and tender. 'I can't believe that only a short time ago I didn't know you…and now look where we are!'

They chinked glasses again, and then he leant forward and took Christa's hand. 'And now I want to know everything about you—why my mother took you on and when your friendship with Colin Maitland started…'

Christa swirled the champagne in her glass and watched the bubbles rise. She smiled and shrugged. 'Not much to tell, really,' she began. 'I'd been away for a long time, at med school and then doing my GP training. I returned to Errin Bridge because my mother had had a mastectomy and my father had died. I wanted desperately to be near her, but jobs for GPs weren't plentiful as there was only one medical centre in the village. I didn't want to work miles away, and in desperation I went to your mother to see if she needed anyone.'

Lachlan watched Christa intently. 'And? Did she take you on immediately?'

'She seemed a bit cautious at first. Said she'd think about it. I'm so glad that she did!'

'You obviously got on well.'

Christa smiled in reminiscence. 'Oh, yes! She had a great sense of humour—she was always telling me to find a man! And the irony was that four years ago she took on Colin Maitland.'

Lachlan nodded. 'Ah, the charming Colin—he pulled the wool over your eyes, then?'

'And some! Of course I fell for him completely—I thought the feeling was mutual. I made excuses for him when he didn't always turn up when he said he would, when he said he had to go off on long weekends… In short, I was a bloody fool! Gave away my heart too easily, I guess.'

'Still bruised by that?' commented Lachlan lightly.

She laughed and shrugged. 'I've certainly learned a few lessons…' Then she added softly, 'But it was Isobel who saved me. She was incredibly kind, told Colin he'd have to find another job. If…if it hadn't been for her, I don't think I could have coped.'

'Of course you would! My mother was obviously very fond of you too—I know she would be pleased that we'd got together.'

Christa grinned. 'Perhaps. On the other hand, she might have thought you were completely mad to start something with me!'

The scallops arrived, steaming and succulent in the light wine sauce, and suddenly Christa felt ravenously hungry.

She looked at Lachlan impishly. 'This looks better than omelettes,' she murmured.

'Nothing will ever outdo the omelette you made for me that night,' he remarked, his eyes twinkling. Then he added, 'By the way, you haven't forgotten that you offered to give me some ideas about doing up Ardenleigh. This weekend?'

'Of course—but not this weekend. I'm at a conference in Inverness on cardiovascular disease.'

'Sounds pretty riveting,' he teased. 'Come a week on Sunday, then. Would that be OK?'

'I'll be there,' she promised.

He leaned towards her, his hand behind her neck, and kissed her softly on her full lips. 'Something to look forward to then…' he murmured.

Paolo bustled up to their table solicitously, beaming at them both. 'Excuse me, *signor, signorina*, a little something from the sweet trolley now? Tiramisu, pannacotta or a delicious gelato perhaps?'

'Just a cappuccino for me,' said Christa. 'I couldn't manage another bite of food!'

'And then home…' whispered Lachlan.

Christa looked at him shrewdly—he had that mischievous twinkle in his eye that revealed what he was anticipating when they got home! And how wonderful it would be to tumble into bed with him and make love. Wasn't she longing for a rerun of the other night? Then that cautious inner voice warned her to be careful—was this going to become the norm, that after an evening out they went to bed together? That was how she and Colin had started—a mad affair that in the end had left her bereft. Surely she'd learned to tread more carefully this time…

She looked at him mock-sternly. 'Don't get too many ideas, Lachlan Maguire. That night we had together was meant to be a one-off!'

'Point taken,' he said, with a wicked grin. 'No harm in trying, though!'

And Christa surmised that he might be chary—not because he was afraid of a broken heart but because he didn't want things to get too serious—whereas she could feel she was already on the threshold of tipping into that thrilling roller-coaster of being headlong in love that she hadn't felt for so long…and it was wonderful.

Christa rested back in her chair and yawned after a busy afternoon dealing with everything from sore backs to chickenpox, and her thoughts drifted happily back to her evening with Lachlan at Matelli's. Despite the fact that she was sure Lachlan was a fair way off a long-term commitment in their relationship, she had a little bubble of elation inside her that made everyday irritations fade into minor blips.

She grinned when she recalled Ginny coming into her room that morning with a face like doom.

'Everything's happened this morning,' she'd intoned gloomily. 'The computer's crashed and the man can't come until lunchtime. We're going to be in chaos.'

Whereas normally Christa might have shared Ginny's frustration, somehow today it hadn't seemed to be such a disaster. 'Oh, well,' she'd remarked serenely. 'We'll just have to go by the manual diary until he comes.'

'And the cleaner's just walked out. Where on earth will we get someone else at short notice?'

'Don't worry!' Christa had said gaily. 'I'll ask my neighbour—she runs an agency. I'm sure she'll find someone.'

Ginny had frowned as if unconvinced and pursued her pessimistic theme. 'And this month's figures on non-attenders are worse than ever. What are we going to do about that? Ben wants to discuss it with you.'

Christa had smiled. 'Oh…we'll put a notice up warning people we may have to ask them to pay if they don't give us notice of non-attendance. We may not be able to carry it out, but it might frighten them!'

Ginny pursed her lips, looking at Christa suspiciously. 'You don't seem terribly bothered—it's not like you to take it all so well. Usually you hit the roof!'

'Oh, well—no good worrying, is it?' Christa had declared blithely. 'We'll work it out!'

Ginny had sighed heavily as if she couldn't understand Christa's casual attitude and had stomped out. She liked to keep on top of all problems! Dear old Ginny—she'd be having a good chunter with Alice about the doctor's irresponsible manner. But that's how being on the edge of love made you, Christa had thought—rather carefree—and after all the sadness of Isobel's death, it was lovely to feel that way!

Now, at the end of the day, Alice came in with a cup of coffee and glancing at Christa's happy expression said rather pityingly, 'I'm afraid I'm going to wipe that beaming smile off your face, Christa. You've got another patient to round off the day. Mrs Donnington, of all people. She's been slotted in this afternoon as an emergency—wouldn't you know it would be her?'

Christa took a grateful sip of coffee and said mildly, 'But that's what I'm here for, Alice! I'm her sounding board, you know. Mrs Donnington may be a pain in the neck sometimes, but part of her trouble is that she's lonely and has no one to talk to.'

Mrs Donnington was a widow, a 'frequent attender', convinced that she suffered from myriad health issues, continually worrying about her health but never with anything specific wrong with her.

'But she comes in nearly every week—she's taking up another poorly patient's place,' protested Alice.

'Even so,' said Christa lightly. 'I can assure you the one time we don't give Mrs Donnington an appointment will be the time she'll have emergency appendicitis. We ignore her at our peril!'

Alice grinned, unrepentant. 'Not much chance of ignoring her. I'm afraid she's got a complaint—other than her health, of course…'

Christa laughed. 'Well, what is it this time?'

'She feels she's been put to the back of the queue today—calls it "discrimination". She wanted to be fitted in this morning—she said an afternoon appointment was highly inconvenient and she'd miss a very important meeting. I offered her one tomorrow, but she said it was too urgent for that.'

Alice went out, clutching a pile of post, and Christa pressed the call system button that lit up the board in the waiting room, calling the next patient.

Amanda Donnington, elderly, but tall and imposing, came into the room and sat down heavily in the chair, pulling off her scarf and sounding rather breathless.

'At last, Doctor! I've been in such discomfort, and this seems to be the only appointment

I could get today, although I wanted to come this morning.'

'Tell me what the problem is,' said Christa kindly.

Mrs Donnington fixed her with a steely glare. 'Of course the main problem is that this place is dangerously understaffed. Since Dr Isobel died it's been nigh impossible to get an appointment on the day one wants. It's been chaos!'

Don't I know it, thought Christa wryly. She smiled at Mrs Donnington pleasantly. 'At least you're being seen today, and you'll be pleased to know we've got another doctor in the practice now.'

'Ah! About time! Perhaps urgent cases won't be pushed to the back of the queue now! Do I know this doctor?'

'He's Dr Lachlan Maguire, Dr Isobel's son.'

Mrs Donnington's expression livened up. 'Really? So he's turned up after all these years. Funny how he left his poor mother so suddenly and never a word from him…'

Christa butted in hastily before her patient

could give her thoughts about that. 'Please, tell me what's worrying you.'

'Oh, I suppose you'll say it's nothing to worry about—that's the usual response I get,' remarked Mrs Donnington rather sourly. 'I've been trying to cope with it for as long as possible, Dr Lennox, knowing how stretched you are, but eventually I've had to give in. Sleep has eluded me completely. I shall need sleeping pills.'

'Where is the discomfort, Mrs Donnington?' asked Christa patiently.

'It's this cough I have—all night, no respite.'

'How long have you had it?'

'On and off for a while. I didn't mention it when I came in last week because it wasn't so bad. But it's got worse. And I'm so sweaty at night. It's extremely uncomfortable.'

Christa looked at Mrs Donnington more closely. She certainly didn't look as robust as usual, paler and perhaps slightly thinner in the face. Somewhere alarm bells rang.

'Have you lost weight, Mrs Donnington?'

'I don't believe in this obsession with weighing oneself—but clothes do seem a little looser, I have to admit.'

'You aren't a smoker, are you?'

'Certainly not, a filthy habit. I'm afraid my dear husband was a chain smoker. I could never persuade him to give up.' A genuine look of sadness crossed Mrs Donnington's face. 'And of course he died of a smoking-related illness, a few years ago now.'

Christa took out her stethoscope. 'I think I'd better have a listen in to your chest.'

A few minutes later, with the examination done, Christa sat down in her chair and looked thoughtfully at her patient. She didn't want to alarm her unnecessarily, but for once Mrs Donnington's trip to the doctor's had been very necessary. The decreased breath sounds and unusual lung noises with areas of dullness in the lung were symptoms that could not be ignored.

Apprehension flickered across Mrs Donnington's face. 'Is something wrong, Doctor?'

'You've certainly got signs of loss of lung function—possibly an infection, for which I'll give you an antibiotic—but given your shortness of breath, night sweats and possible weight loss, I'd like to send you to the chest clinic at St Luke's Hospital.'

Mrs Donnington turned pale. 'The…the hospital?'

Christa leaned forward in her chair and smiled reassuringly. 'I want to make sure we cover every possibility, and I can't do all the tests here or give you a chest X-ray. But you've done absolutely the right thing coming to me…'

'You think I've got lung cancer, don't you?'

'Not necessarily. Your symptoms could have many reasons—but we need to cover every possibility. Of course it's my job to investigate your problem, and if I'm not sure of a diagnosis to send you to a consultant who specialises in everything to do with lungs. I'm sure you agree with me, don't you?'

Mrs Donnington suddenly looked smaller and frailer. Most of the many times she'd come to see the doctor her complaints had been trivial and her worries had always been allayed—now she was having to face the reality that she could be really ill.

Christa watched Mrs Donnington with compassion as the woman tried to assimilate the unexpected news that her complaint could be more serious than an irritating cough. There would be shock, physical as well as mental, a feeling of being out of control, even panic.

'I don't want you to think the worst, Mrs Donnington,' Christa said gently. 'More often than not these things turn out to be run-of-the-mill symptoms that have no sinister cause. Now, why don't you go and have a coffee with your daughter? Doesn't she live near you?'

Mrs Donnington got out of her chair slowly, clutching her enormous handbag, and gave a nervous laugh. 'Oh, I don't think so… Verity leads a very demanding life, you see, what with taking the children backwards and forwards and dealing with her horses. We don't seem to have time to see each other very often, and, as she says, the weekend is the only time she gets to herself.'

And that's one of the clues to the cause of Amanda Donnington's loneliness, thought Christa, looking at the sad expression on the woman's face and wondering how much the woman's grandchildren featured in her life. Without knowing Verity, Christa surmised that an elderly woman who might be bossy, interfering and possibly rather needy, could be sidelined from the daughter's life.

She smiled sympathetically. 'Well, treat yourself to something at the local café! I'm going to ask for an early hospital appointment, which should be in a few days. You won't have long to wait.'

Mrs Donnington nodded, her imperious manner diminished. 'Thank you, Doctor. Thank you for seeing me.' Then added with more spirit, 'I knew there was something wrong!'

And that, thought Christa wryly, was a very good example of why every patient should be listened to carefully. She wrote an e-mail to St. Luke's lung and chest department, asking for an urgent appointment for Mrs Donnington.

She closed down the computer and picked up her handbag, wishing like mad that she'd be seeing Lachlan that weekend, instead of sitting through two days of lectures on tackling cardiovascular disease.

CHAPTER EIGHT

AFTER THE STUFFY gloom of the lecture hall it took Christa a second or two to adjust to the bright light in the huge reception area. All around her people were jostling and chattering, relieved to stretch their legs after a long stint listening to the professor's rather expressionless voice expounding on the benefits of the early diagnosis of hypertension.

A small plump figure with blonde hair materialised in front of her, and a cheery voice said, 'I don't believe it. Christa Lennox! I never thought I'd see you here!'

Christa stared in surprise at the smiling face. 'Suzy Collins, as I live and breathe!' she gasped. 'I thought you were in Australia!'

'Not any more I'm not! I'm married and doing anaesthetics near Glasgow now.'

The two women embraced and Suzy stepped

back and surveyed her old friend admiringly. 'You look better than ever, Christa—hardly changed at all after nearly ten years. I thought a few years in the hard world of work would age you!'

'Is it that long since we shared a house at uni?' Christa laughed. 'God, have we got some catching up to do! Let's have lunch and forget about hypertension and cardiac problems for a while.'

They made their way to the canteen and sat down at a side table.

'So,' said Suzy. 'What's it like, working up in the Highlands?'

Christa gave her a quick résumé of her life at Errin Bridge, and told her of Isobel Maguire's tragic death.

'Isobel Maguire?' repeated Suzy with a frown. 'Not Lachlan Maguire's mother?'

'You know him?' asked Christa in surprise.

'I met him in Sydney when we were first looking for jobs. We kept bumping into each other—he always had some glamorous bird in tow!'

Christa's heart did a double thump. 'I suppose he had lots of girlfriends,' she said lightly.

Suzy chuckled. 'You don't get a hunky guy like him being stuck for female company. But he was always very careful not to get tied down—you know what I mean? I knew him quite well and we used to have the odd coffee together—nothing romantic between us, I was otherwise engaged! He used to tease me, saying he couldn't understand people getting hitched for life—he liked to have variety!'

'Oh, he did, did he?' Christa forced herself to laugh, but Suzy's description seemed to be an accurate portrayal of what Lachlan had said, so it shouldn't surprise her.

'Too right! Many girls tried to catch him, but he wouldn't be tied down. So, honey, you be careful around young Maguire,' teased Suzy.

'I certainly will.' Christa smiled, but her casual words hid her firm intention to be very careful indeed when it came to dating Lachlan. Everything Suzy had said seemed to confirm what he was like. Then she changed the subject and they talked of the happy times they'd had together as students, and what had happened to all their friends.

'It's been so good seeing you,' said Suzy when they'd finished lunch. 'Let's get together very soon. We mustn't lose touch again. I'd love you to meet Pete, my husband. He's looking after the kids at the moment, so I'll be dashing off after this afternoon's stint.'

And for the rest of the weekend Christa seemed to hear Suzy's words about Lachlan echoing round in her head. 'He couldn't understand people getting hitched for life!' A gypsy's warning, perhaps?

Christa had barely seen Lachlan since their evening out at Matelli's As they had arranged then, the Sunday following the conference she was to go over to Ardenleigh with her ideas on decorating the house.

When the day came she was delighted to see that after a week of dull, cold weather it was a beautiful sparkling day. She pulled on a fleece over her T-shirt and jogging pants, and Titan bounded up, full of joy at the anticipation of a long walk.

'Come on, then, Titan—we'll see Mum before we go to Lachlan's.'

The little dog gave a bark of approval and trotted cheerfully alongside Christa as she set off. The crisp air was as heady as champagne, and she took deep breaths as she ran along the lane towards her mother's flat, feeling the release of tension as she worked her body hard after a week's arduous work. There was a light hoar frost on the verges, and it clung to the trees and hedges, glittering in the morning sun—everywhere looked magical.

Her thoughts went like a magnet to Lachlan. Indeed, it had been difficult to get him out of her mind since that magical night when he'd come over for a meal. In moments when she wasn't busy, her imagination worked overtime, feeling the firmness of his mouth kissing her lips, his skilful hands caressing her and the strength and warmth of his fit, lean body against hers. She'd almost come to the conclusion that she would never again feel attracted to any man. But after only a short acquaintance with Lachlan, everything in her body and mind was revitalised—

she felt alive, energised and free of all the sad memories of the past.

She was tremendously happy—of course she was! She was going to be spending most of Sunday with Lachlan. He'd suggested lunch and a walk after they'd discussed the colour schemes and alterations he might try at Ardenleigh.

Christa tried to push to the back of her mind any possibility that she might be stupid enough to fall madly in love with a man who only wanted a brief encounter. Suzy's words still echoed in her head, and it would be a sure-fire way to having her heart broken again.

This heady feeling of happiness wasn't love—of course it couldn't be. She'd only known the man a matter of weeks. But it was certainly an overwhelming attraction. She was going to play it cool, make sure that the only exercise they did would be that brisk walk and forbid herself to think their relationship would go on for ever! She didn't want a rerun of her experience with Colin.

She turned into the drive that led to the block

of flats in which her mother lived and knocked on the door, which was on the latch.

'Mum? Are you there?' she called. 'I've just dropped in for a moment to make sure you're OK.'

She heard the murmur of voices in the lounge and went into where her mother was sitting with Bertie, her friend from the next-door flat.

Pat came over to kiss her. 'Darling—how lovely of you to come over. Have you run here? How trim you look! I wondered if you'd have time to see me this weekend, you being so busy at the moment.'

Bertie, tall and military looking, bent down to stroke Titan. 'Grand little dog, this,' he said. 'If we weren't in a flat I'd have one just like him.'

'You can always borrow him.' Christa smiled. 'How are you, Bertie—your angina not troubling you at the moment?'

Bertie was a patient of hers and had had a few episodes of angina over the past few years.

'Absolutely fine. Those pills work a treat.'

'Well, don't forget to come in for your check-up soon. Are you off somewhere nice today?'

'We're just off to Marfield House—it's that stately home in the hills. We'll have a little walk in the grounds and a coffee. I'm so glad it's not raining, everything looks so much better in the sun.' Pat looked assessingly at her daughter. 'Talking of looking better, you look one hundred per cent less stressed and tired than the last time I saw you. This Lachlan Maguire must be pulling his weight. Is he proving an asset?'

'It's a tremendous help, having him there.'

'So you like him, then?'

Christa suppressed a giggle but kept her voice light. 'He's a good doctor—no worries about that.' She paused for a second and then remarked easily, 'Perhaps you ought to meet him some time.'

Her mother smiled. 'Maybe, one day—there's no hurry, I'm sure,' she said lightly. 'And you? What are you doing today? Having a rest, I hope.'

'Well, I'm on my way to see Lachlan, as a matter of fact. I said I'd help him with some ideas for doing up Ardenleigh. He says he hasn't a clue!'

Pat looked at her sharply and took a deep

breath. 'Look, darling, I know you'll think I'm interfering, but it's just a bit of advice. Please, be careful, won't you? After your previous experience you must know that sometimes working closely with someone can lead to...well, you know, working with a colleague is one thing, but socialising is another...'

Christa sighed. 'I've told you, Mum, I shall be very careful. And I'm bound to see him outside working hours anyway.'

Pat shook her head and pursed her lips, and Christa said impatiently, 'Oh, for goodness' sake, Mum! What have you got against Lachlan? You don't know him! The episode with Colin is history now, anyway.' She looked at her mother's expression and frowned. 'Is it Lachlan or men in general you're not keen on?'

Pat looked flustered and rather forlorn. 'Darling...it's just that... Oh, dear, let's not come to blows about it. I shouldn't have said anything. You're a big girl now—I suppose I forget that sometimes!'

Christa gave her mother a quick hug. 'I know you do, Mum!'

But as she left the flat Christa recalled her mother's less-than-enthusiastic words about Isobel the other day. What was it about the Maguire family that made her mother uneasy? she wondered. Then she shrugged to herself—there had to be a reason for her mother's anxiety and one day she'd get to the bottom of it, but for the immediate future she had more interesting things to do. She felt a flicker of excited anticipation as she started running down the lane towards Ardenleigh.

Lachlan was hacking away at huge overgrown laurels by the front door, and for the first time in years the beautiful golden stonework was beginning to appear. His hair was dishevelled, and he was wearing an old tartan lumber jacket over battered cord trousers—he looked strong and utterly gorgeous, as virile as someone in an advertisement for an unbelievably effective tonic!

When he saw her, he flung down his secateurs and strode over to her, sliding his arms round her waist, his hands spread across her back so that she was imprisoned against him. Christa's vow to distance herself from him seemed to disintegrate like bubbles floating in the air, and she found herself winding her arms round his neck, desperate to be as close to him as she could, to feel him against her once again. He buried his face in her hair and kissed her neck softly.

'Mmm…you smell so sweet,' he murmured. 'I've nearly gone crazy waiting for you to turn up…wanting to hold you.'

His hand crept under her T-shirt, cupping her breast gently, and a whoosh of sensation thrilled through her. Any second now it would be a complete rerun of the other night!

With a tremendous effort of will Christa managed to disentangle herself from Lachlan and, half laughing, managed to gasp, 'Hey, not so fast, young man! And anyway,' she said primly, 'we agreed that what we did the other night, was just a bit of fun, a one-off, didn't we?'

Lachlan raised his eyebrows. 'Is that all it meant to you?' he said lightly. 'I obviously didn't make much of an impression! I'll have to make more of an effort next time!' he said with a grin.

She pushed him away with a giggle. 'We've got work to do! I've brought the sample paint pots.'

He looked down at her, surprised. 'The what? Oh…' He threw back his head and laughed. 'Good God, girl, I wasn't thinking about paint then. I was thinking… Oh, what the hell, come in and let's have some coffee while I tell you what I was thinking about!'

It was like an invitation from the spider to the fly, thought Christa wryly. There was no way she could regard him as purely a work colleague when the man exuded sex from every pore, and no way she could resist that invitation!

The percolator was already bubbling quietly away and there was a delicious smell of fresh coffee pervading the place. Lachlan poured some out into mugs for them both and put them on the table, then turned to her and put his hands on her shoulders,

'Now I'll tell you what I was thinking of…' he said with a cheeky grin, dipping his head to hers and brushing her mouth softly, then gradually his kissing became more demanding, teasing her lips apart, moving his hands over her body. With commendable willpower, Christa wriggled free of him for a second time and he stepped back, his blue eyes dancing with amusement.

'What's the matter?' he asked innocently. 'Am I doing something wrong?'

Christa tried to look severe, and smothered another giggle. 'If you want me to help you with advice about the house, you'd better not do that,' she said crisply. 'It seems to drive any sensible idea out of my head!'

'You're so bossy,' grumbled Lachlan. 'But don't imagine it's out of the question that I won't try again!' He handed her a mug of coffee and they sat in a companionable way on the wooden kitchen chairs next to each other. 'So how was your conference—a lot of laughs?'

'I met an old friend of yours there.' She smiled. 'She told me all about you!'

Lachlan looked startled. 'Who could that be?'

'Suzy Collins—she knew you in Australia.'

'Ah, Suzy! Great fun…' He looked suspiciously at Christa. 'I hope she didn't give away any state secrets…'

Christa smiled demurely. 'Nothing I didn't know about you already!'

He laughed. 'Then I can relax. Let's get back to business. Tell me what you think about the kitchen, for a start.'

Christa looked around—he'd made an attempt to clear the place of all the old bottles and cans that she'd seen on the shelves the first night he'd arrived, and he'd stripped the floor of the battered linoleum that had been there before. The old green-painted doors on the cupboards had been taken off and were piled on the kitchen table.

'You've been working hard—it looks better already!'

'You should have seen some of the stuff in those jars! I think there was a good supply of penicillin growing on top of some of them!'

'So are you going to strip the doors or paint them again?'

'I don't know… What do you suggest?'

'I think I'd like to see the original pine or perhaps spray them cream. Lighten things up a little.' She peered through a half-open door at the side of the kitchen. 'What's through there?'

'A very cold scullery with two sinks in it—I suppose it's what used to be called a wash-house.'

Christa went to inspect it and laughed. 'It's too tiny to be of much use—you could always knock down the wall and make the kitchen bigger. And then you could make a huge picture window here, overlooking a lovely view of the garden.'

Lachlan looked enthusiastic. 'Yeah, that would look great. I suppose we could even have huge glass sliding doors the length of that wall…'

Was it a Freudian slip that he said 'we could have'? wondered Christa wistfully. Then she told herself crossly that he had no notions of including her in his plans—he just wanted advice. He led her to the front of the house and into the drawing room.

'What about this room?' he said.

It was a magnificent room with two huge bay windows on either side of French doors, which flooded the place with light. But there was the musty, damp smell of a room never aired, never lived in. At one end of the room there was an enormous fireplace that cried out for a log fire on a winter's day such as this. In her imagination Christa saw the cheerful flicker of flames shooting up the chimney, could smell the sweet smell of applewood, picture the two of them in front of it, doing wonderful things to each other… She veered quickly away from that daydream—it was becoming almost a reflex reaction that when she thought of Lachlan she thought of making love!

'You need to warm this room up,' she suggested briskly, forcing that image out of her mind. 'Have you any wood to make up a fire in that fireplace?'

'Plenty. I was cutting some from the front when you came. We'll do it later after we've been out.'

'And you know what? That peeling wallpaper should be easy to pull down, and it would look fabulous with a lovely soft green wash over the walls! And if you got rid of this old carpet and put down a new one—say, pale oatmeal, it would set off the lovely old oak furniture in here.'

Christa looked at the sagging and faded settee and matching chairs, and the curtains, sadly fraying, exposed as they were to the sunlight.

'And another thing,' she continued brightly, 'if you went to the country house sales around here, you could easily buy a new settee and chairs, and curtains, and if….'

Lachlan grinned and put up his hand. 'Whoa! Steady!' he remarked. 'We're talking serious money here. Remember, the stuff I'm short of?'

'I hadn't forgotten that. Talking of which…' She took a deep breath and said boldly, 'I suppose you haven't had second thoughts about the leisure development?'

He laughed. 'You don't give up, do you?' He leant against the wall, his legs casually crossed, hands in pockets. 'Actually, I've had a lot of interest and early signs are that the council isn't against it in principle.'

Christa's expression turned to one of determination. 'Well, when the planning application comes up, I can assure you that several of us will be objecting to that in the strongest terms.'

Lachlan looked at her from under his brow. 'Look, don't let's argue about it. Why don't we have that walk now while the sun's out? We'll go down to the beach through the woods and fields and I can show you exactly what the plan might be.' He stepped forward and put his arms round her, tilting her face to his, and said impishly, 'Who knows? Perhaps I can persuade you to change your mind.'

He smiled down at her, those blue eyes of his exuding sex. He took her face in his hands and kissed her lingeringly, and she turned her face away, half laughing, half irritated that he should joke about something so important to her.

'That's an unfair tactic,' she protested.

'All's fair in love and war,' he commented, taking her hand and going through to the kitchen, opening the back door and striding down the garden towards the woods and fields.

Titan bounded energetically before them, barking furiously at imaginary rabbits, and Christa felt a sudden surge of elation because she was alone with Lachlan on a beautiful day, and had a chance to get to know him better. Surely it was the start of a relationship that would go further than a light-hearted affair, and even if Lachlan protested that long-term commitment was not for him, perhaps one day he'd see some merit in it!

They came to the wood that bordered the fields and Lachlan stopped and put a hand on Christa's shoulders, pointing to a part of the wood that wasn't so densely treed.

'The company that wants to buy the land intends to have about eight wooden chalets here—and they'll be made Swedish-style with wood that blends in with the surroundings,' he explained. 'No huge buildings, and the minimum amount of tree felling.'

'And what about the leisure centre itself, with the swimming pool and gym? That will be hard to disguise surely?'

'Same idea—a wooden structure on one floor and to the far side of the wood, so it won't be seen from the house or the road.'

He was good at the talk, thought Christa. He made it sound as if no one would notice any difference to the place at all, and indeed it didn't seem so very intrusive despite what she'd imagined.

She murmured, 'I have no doubt it will be very popular with holiday people—it's in such a beautiful area. But you haven't quite convinced me yet.'

He grinned and bent down to kiss the nape of her neck. 'That's a challenge—I've every confidence I can win you over!' He took her hand. 'Now, let's take Titan down to the beach and you can look back at it from that angle.'

They walked briskly through the furrowed fields, swinging hands, and came to the line of sand dunes that marked the edge of the beach. It spread gloriously before them, wide, empty and pearly pink, and the sun sparkled on the sea, millpond smooth but with little waves like lace ruffling the shallows. Above them mewed the seagulls, swooping and gliding before settling on the water. To the right of the firth were the hazy outlines of the Cairngorms, already white-tipped with early snow against a wintry blue sky.

'Isn't this perfect?' Lachlan murmured, folding his arms and standing in mute admiration of the scene for a few minutes.

'Better than Australia, then?' teased Christa. 'What made you go so far away when you love it so much here—and for so long?'

'Good question.' He shrugged. 'Obviously it was an adventure, a marvellous opportunity to see the world—but would I have gone at that particular time if my mother hadn't told me about her affair? I don't know… All I do know is that I wanted to get as far away as I could from my family.'

'You'd qualified by then?' probed Christa.

'Yes, thank God. At least I could earn my living at something. And I loved it—the people, the country and the experience. The variety of stuff I had to tackle was like *Casualty* on a grand scale—snake bites, dysentery, dehydration. It all made for a quick learning curve.'

She grinned cheekily at him. 'I'm surprised you can contemplate coming back to work in the practice if you loved it so much.' Then she added gently, 'But it must have been a terrible shock when you heard Isobel had died.'

His face shadowed sadly. 'I haven't talked about it before, but I admit it was a hammer blow.' He sighed and bunched his fists in his trouser pockets, staring across the firth. 'I'm ashamed to say that I actually felt resentful, as if it was my poor mother's fault she'd died so suddenly that I was unable to make my peace with her.'

Christa nodded. 'That's understandable.'

Lachlan shrugged. 'During the time I've been back my feelings have changed—I feel guilty as hell that I left it so long to come home. I'd kept thinking I should return, but I suppose I was too proud to meet my mother again—apologise for what I had said to her. And now it's too late...'

His voice died away, the sad words hanging in the air, filled with poignancy. Christa reached for his hand and squeezed it comfortingly, aware of the effort it was taking for Lachlan to admit his mistakes.

'I'm sure she forgave you, Lachlan, probably understood only too well why you left home. I'm sure she felt guilty too, breaking up the family.'

'Yes,' he said softly. 'She did forgive me—she

left a letter with the solicitor that made it plain that she blamed herself for all that happened.' He was silent for a moment then looked bleakly at Christa. 'Now I realise that she was well aware that her time was short, and if I could only turn back the clock, I would. I regret so much not making it up with my mother. One thing I do know,' he added fiercely, 'is that I shall do everything I can to fulfil her wishes in that letter. At least I can do that!'

There was something heartbreaking about seeing his strong face etched with sadness and the remorse he felt about being too late to make amends with his mother. Christa put her arm around him and hugged him to her.

'None of it was of your making. You thought you had an idyllic family life with parents who loved each other. It must have shattered you when you realised that wasn't true.' She hesitated before saying diffidently, 'Did your mother's affair end when your father left home?'

'Her lover was killed in a crash on the motorway,' Lachlan said simply. 'I hoped it would mean she and my father would get back together but they didn't and he left the area.' He gave a short, bitter laugh. 'So much for that ridiculous vow to be together till death did them part.'

Was that shorthand for reminding her that he did not believe in commitment for life? wondered Christa wistfully. She remembered his throwaway remark: 'Marry in haste, repent at leisure.' Wedding bells didn't seem to be on his agenda!

He put his hands on her shoulders and smiled. 'God, this is all about me, me, me! Now, let's get comfortable and tell me about your family—your mother…'

And by 'comfortable' he evidently meant that they should sit together on the soft sand in the dunes, one arm around her, hugging her to him. She snuggled up to him, loving the feel of his warm body against hers.

'Ah…Mum's one feisty woman,' she said. 'She was devastated after Dad's death, but gradually she's developed plenty of interests—and, of course, now she has her friend Bertie, the loveliest man from the next-door flat, and they do loads of things together.'

Lachlan grinned. 'A feisty woman, eh? You sound as if you take after her. I'd like to meet your mother. I take it your father wasn't a medical man?'

'No. He used to run a small business with my Uncle Angus, supplying drugs to medical practices, although sadly in later years apparently they didn't get on. But my father was lovely, great fun and I do miss him…'

'He was different from your wicked uncle Angus, then?' Lachlan said lightly. 'What happened to Angus's wife and child after he left them?'

'I believe she moved away down south and remarried. We never hear from her unfortunately. You said you'd met him—did he seem wicked to you?'

Lachlan hesitated for a second then said, 'He did have a reputation with women, I suppose…'

'How could you tell?' she asked, smiling.

He pushed his hand through his thick hair so that it stood up in little spikes, and looked at Christa quizzically. 'There's rather more to your uncle's story than you might imagine…'

She looked surprised and laughed. ‘Oh? That’s very intriguing.’

‘Could be a bit of a shock.’

‘Nothing much shocks me. Spill the beans, I’m a big girl now!’ Fleetingly, she remembered that she’d said as much to her mother a few hours earlier.

Lachlan shrugged. ‘Hell. You’ve got to know some time. Are you ready for this?’ He paused as if weighing up how to tell Christa, then said, with a trace of bitterness, ‘The fact is, the man my mother had an affair with was your uncle. Angus Lennox used to come to the surgery as a drug rep for his company—and that’s how he met my mother. The rest is history. Then he was killed in a traffic accident coming to see her one evening, but by that time her marriage was over, and so was our happy family life.’

CHAPTER NINE

THE SMILE FADED from Christa's face and she gazed at Lachlan in complete amazement, her mouth an O of surprise.

'*What?* Isobel and Uncle Angus? You're kidding!' She pulled some long grass from the sand dune and pulled at it distractedly. 'I can hardly believe it. Isobel and I were so close, but she never gave a hint that she'd had an affair, let alone that it was with Angus…'

'Reopening old wounds, do you think?' suggested Lachlan gently.

Christa nodded. 'Perhaps… But it's such a shock.'

She bit her lip, suddenly realising just why her mother seemed less than enthusiastic about Isobel, and a relationship developing between her daughter and Lachlan.

So *that* was what had caused the huge rift between her father and his brother—brothers who had been so close before Angus's affair. That closeness had been severed for ever after he'd left his wife and had then died, and the unhappy memories of that time must still rankle with her mother.

She got up from beside Lachlan and walked over to the little stone breakwater at the edge of the dunes, and Lachlan stood beside her and put his arm round her. 'I'm sorry I had to tell you, sweetheart, but surely it's better that you know…'

'Of course I should know,' she said robustly. 'I can't imagine why Mum kept it to herself all these years—it certainly makes things a little clearer.'

'How do you mean?'

'I've always felt that she was never as, well, fond of Isobel as I was.' She hesitated before saying in a rather embarrassed way, 'And when I told her you were joining the practice she didn't seem exactly keen.'

He raised his eyebrows. 'But these things

happened a long time ago, honey. Surely she's moved on from there by now?'

She sighed. 'Perhaps.' She looked at Lachlan with a frown. 'But you must have hated our family too. No wonder you seemed startled when you heard who I was—the niece of the man who had broken up your parents' marriage working with your mother! That's a big crumb to swallow.'

'It was a shock at first,' Lachlan admitted, then his deep blue eyes held hers and he said with a cheeky grin, 'Now I don't think that way at all, I can tell you—especially after that wonderful night we had together, sweetheart!'

He turned her round gently and tilted her face to his, then brushed her mouth with a feather touch of his lips, trailing kisses down her neck. It was unbearably sexy, sending sparks of desire through every nerve of her body, dissolving her legs to jelly, making her feel dizzy with desire—and it took every ounce of control for Christa to pull herself back from him, half laughing, half protesting.

'Oh, Lachlan—stop it! I just want you to understand how much that quarrel between my uncle and my father affected my family. I can see why Mum would resent any connection to the Maguires.'

'That's ridiculous!' The wind blew Lachlan's hair over his eyes and he brushed it away impatiently. 'Surely she doesn't harbour a grudge against me. After all, it wasn't *my* fault!' He looked down at her with a grin. 'Mind you, I won't deny it was a shock to learn when I arrived back here a few weeks ago that you were Angus Lennox's niece. I even felt a twang of jealousy that you and my mother had this terrific bond when you worked together. But it's history now...'

Christa looked at him levelly. 'I could never risk upsetting Mum, Lachlan. It's just been the two of us for so long and she sacrificed such a lot to get me through med school. Can you understand that? I need to tread carefully.'

'So what are you saying, Christa? That it affects your relationship with me?'

Lachlan's blue eyes glowered down at her truculently, and she was silent for a moment. Did it really make a difference to her relationship with Lachlan? Would she reopen old wounds of her mother's by going out with him? Perhaps it was better to put the brakes on a budding romance before it got too serious—on her side anyway.

'It changes things a little…' she said at last.

'But surely you're not going to be ruled by your mother all your life? Why should you be constrained by what she thinks?' He sounded exasperated.

Christa flushed. 'Because she *is* my mother! I just happen to care about her feelings—that's all.'

'I never thought of you as a mummy's girl,' he commented drily.

A cold wind blew across the firth and the temperature between them seemed to drop as well—what had started out as a magical day suddenly seemed dark.

Christa's eyes flashed angrily. 'Don't be so ridiculous! I'm just saying that falling out with my mother is something I could never do!'

Lachlan's expression hardened and he said

tersely, 'If that's supposed to be a sanctimonious dig at me and my relationship with Isobel, it's a cheap jibe!'

'You know I didn't mean it that way!' Christa stared at him coldly. 'I just want to sound the ground a bit…surely you can understand that?'

They gazed stonily at each other, their bodies tense, standing some way apart. Christa shivered, and not just because of the cold wind but because this silly quarrel seemed to have sprung out of nowhere—and it was horrible that one minute they could be so close and the next as if they were on different planets.

Lachlan bunched his fists in his pockets, appalled that the temperature between them had plummeted several degrees below freezing—and, in his view, over nothing at all! The wind had whipped Christa's auburn hair into a tousled halo and her eyes were bright with anger—and she had never looked lovelier. Lachlan's expression softened, and he stepped forward, putting out his arms and drawing her close to him.

'Come here, Christa. What are we like? Of course you care what your mother thinks, and so do I. Go and talk to her—tell her about us. She might not be so against it as you thought. After all, we're just…rather good friends, aren't we?'

Christa swallowed. Of course they were! She was making a fuss over nothing…

He smiled at her, his periwinkle blue eyes heart-meltingly rueful. 'I didn't mean to be so unsympathetic. We'll take things as slowly as you like. Am I forgiven?'

And Christa, nestled into the comfort of that warm body, shook her head, smiling remorsefully up at him. 'Don't be silly! It's my fault. I guess I went over the top a bit. You're right—who I go out with is nothing to do with my mother. But learning the truth about Angus was a tremendous shock. To think I worked all those years with Isobel and she never revealed it.' She dimpled up at him. 'There's no more little secrets you're hiding from me, are there?'

'Only a few,' he murmured. 'Now let me apologise to you properly…'

And apologising took quite a long time, because his lips were on hers demandingly, his hands caressing her body tenderly, and any thoughts she'd had about upsetting her mother seemed gradually to melt away. She would have a talk with her mother some time—that would be the best thing. If Lachlan could get over his aversion to the Lennox family, surely Pat could accept Lachlan.

A few huge drops of rain splashed down onto them and Lachlan glanced up at the sky. Dark clouds were massing over the firth and the wind was whipping up.

'Do you think we could go somewhere more comfortable?' he suggested mildly. 'It's bloody freezing out here and we're going to be soaked! We'll go back to Ardenleigh, and I'll light a fire in that big fireplace in the drawing room, like you suggested. It will be cosy and warm in no time.'

A sudden vivid vision of two bodies in front of the fire, warmed by its heat and entwined together, floated into Christa's mind, sending little sparks of excitement crackling through her body.

She laughed. 'Sounds good to me. But remember what we said about not rushing things…'

Lachlan grinned wickedly. 'I'll give it careful thought,' he said.

Neither of them heard Christa's mobile ringing at first, then Christa grimaced and pulled it out of her pocket.

'Wouldn't you know it—I thought I'd turned it off,' she said.

She held it to her ear and her expression changed. Her mother's agitated voice sounded in her ear. She mouthed to Lachlan, 'It's Mum—she sounds awful…'

'Christa? Oh, darling, something awful's h-happened,' Pat stuttered hoarsely. 'Could you get here as soon as possible? It's Bertie, he's, he's just collapsed with terrible pain across his chest. He says it's just a pulled muscle, but he looks very grey and his breathing seems so laboured…'

Christa's heart froze. Dear God, it sounded as if Bertie was having a heart attack. 'Have you rung for an ambulance, Mum?'

'Yes…then they rang back to say they'd come as quickly as they could, but they've been diverted because of a landslide through the Inchhill Pass. They told me to ring the GP and they'd be there as soon as they could—and to try and prop Bertie up. I've tried to but he's heavy… Oh, dear me…'

There was an edge of panic in her mother's voice, and Christa forced her own voice to be calm. 'I'm on my way now, Mum. Is he at your flat? I'll get in touch with the ambulance service again and see if they've got through the landslide. Don't worry—keep talking to Bertie, reassure him that help's on its way.'

'I get the drift,' said Lachlan, who'd been watching her face intently. 'Come on—let's get your car and your medical bag.'

They sprinted along the sands, the rain and wind beating into their faces.

'It's my mother's elderly neighbour…Bertie Smith,' panted Christa, her words tumbling over each other as she tried to explain what had happened to Lachlan as they ran. 'She thinks he's had a heart attack, and the ambulance is stuck in the Inchhill Pass…'

Dealing with emergencies like this was something GPs had to cope with, but Lachlan was well aware that in a life-and-death situation it could be a blessing to have another pair of hands.

'Have you got adrenalin and morphine in your bag?'

'Yes—and atropine.'

'What about oxygen?'

'Thank God I've got a cylinder in the boot. It's a spare for a patient, but she's got plenty to be going on with.'

'Then while you're driving I'll get an update on the ambulance's ETA.'

They picked up Christa's car and medical bag, and she put her foot down, going as fast as she dared to her mother's flat. Lachlan flicked a glance at her worried face as they sped through the main street of Errin Bridge.

'You know this neighbour of your mother's?'

Christa nodded. 'Yes, he's a friend really as well as being one of our patients. He's actually had angina for a few years, but it seems to have been well under control. He and my mother have been "going out" together for a long time—he's wonderful with Mum and such a sweet man.' She gripped the steering-wheel tightly and said in a small voice, 'I—I'm glad you're here, Lachlan...'

'So am I—two hands are better than one in this case.'

'The truth is,' she said bleakly, 'this seems like a rerun of when your mother died. I was called out to someone who had collapsed at a farm in the hills, and I only knew it was Isobel when I got there. But I was too late…'

There was silence for a minute, the words 'too late' seeming to hang in the air.

Lachlan said softly, 'We can only do our best in these situations, you know—it doesn't always work.'

'I know, I know,' sighed Christa as she swung into the drive of her mother's block of flats.

Bertie was on the floor with a cushion half-propping him up against a chair, his head had fallen to one side, his skin grey and his eyes sunken. Pat was holding his hand and stroking his forehead, her head whipping round when she heard Christa and Lachlan come in.

'Thank God,' she whispered. 'I don't know if he's… It all happened so quickly—one minute we were discussing a holiday, and the next…' Her voice trailed off miserably.

Lachlan bent down by the stricken man and put two fingers on his carotid artery. His eyes met Christa's and he nodded. 'There's still a pulse…clear signs of coronary thrombosis. Have you heparin with you? I'll go and bring in that oxygen while you take over, Christa.'

Bertie's eyes fluttered open, and through purple-tinged lips he whispered, 'It's…it's the pain…'

Lachlan knew that the vice-like grip in Bertie's chest was all the man could think of, pain coursing through his neck and chest, and an increasing sense of losing touch with the world around him. He put his face close to Bertie's ear.

'Don't worry, Bertie—don't try to talk. We know what's happened to you and we're going to sort you out. We'll give you something for the pain.'

His voice was crisp and authoritative, and Christa saw her mother put her hands up to her mouth, eyes wide with fright and riveted to the scene as she watched the two doctors trying to save the life of her friend.

'Will...will he be all right?' she whispered. 'He was fine when we went for our walk—seemed as right as rain. It all happened so suddenly.'

Christa didn't answer. Bertie might still be alive, but his life was on a knife-edge, with the grim prospect of a full cardiac arrest. She listened to Bertie's labouring heart through her stethoscope while she felt the weak, thready pulse on his wrist. Lachlan hooked a mask round Bertie's face and undid a valve in the oxygen cylinder to help the patient's breathing.

'He's bradycardic—heartbeat under sixty,' Christa said succinctly. 'I'm giving him one milligram of atropine to try and stabilise him and bring his heartbeat up, and five thousand units of heparin.'

She slipped off the cover of the syringe and tested it with a small spray in the air before injecting it into the man's arm. They watched him intently, and gradually the colour in Bertie's face began to change from grey to pink as his labouring heart found the capacity to pump blood more efficiently around his body.

Now a cuff was wound round Bertie's upper arm and Christa pressed a stethoscope to the skin below it, and after a few seconds the erratic beat of Bertie's heart began to steady.

She took a long breath and murmured, 'I think we're getting there...he's in sinus rhythm now.' She held Bertie's hand and smiled down at him. 'You're doing well, Bertie—just relax until the paramedics get here.'

Pat watched them from the corner of the room and wiped her eyes. 'I...I'll just go and make some tea for us all,' she said in a trembling voice. She came over to Bertie and bent over him, squeezing his hand and saying softly, 'Don't you ever give me a fright like that again, Bertie Smith, or I'll not talk to you again!'

And Bertie, with his oxygen mask over his face, managed to mouth to her, 'I love you, darling...'

Pat bent down and kissed his cheek, her own cheeks wet with tears. 'I love you too, my sweet. Please...please get better for me.'

Over their heads, Christa and Lachlan's eyes met and held each other's gaze as they smiled at each other.

It wasn't long before the ambulance arrived and Bertie was taken to hospital, with Pat insisting that she go with him.

'I'm not staying here, and I'm not letting Bertie go alone in that ambulance,' she said firmly.

'We'll follow behind,' said Christa.

'No way!' declared Pat, with such a look of Christa's when she was in a bossy mood that Lachlan hid a grin behind his hand. 'I'll get a taxi back—you two need a meal. You've done everything you could—now the hospital can take over.'

'Promise me you'll ring me when he's settled, then…'

Pat held her hand up as if to stop Christa in full flow and said with dignity, 'I want to stay next to Bertie all night if need be—it's kind of you, but I shall come home by taxi and that's an end to it!'

Christa laughed. 'You win!' She looked from

her mother to Lachlan and made a quick decision. 'And, Mum, I haven't had time to introduce you to Lachlan Maguire. As I told you, he's working with me now.'

She watched her mother's face as she made the introduction. Pat hesitated for just a fraction of a second then put her hand out to shake Lachlan's with a smile of genuine warmth. 'I can't tell you how grateful I am—and pleased to meet you. Thank you so much for saving Bertie's life. I shall always be in yours and Christa's debt!'

The ambulance took them off and Christa and Lachlan were left standing together in the dark, watching the taillights disappear down the road.

'Well, well, what a wonderful thing love is,' murmured Lachlan. 'It looks as if your mother's found someone she loves very much."

Christa took a deep breath and said softly, 'I'm sure Mum didn't realise that she loved Bertie so much until this happened. Seeing him at the brink of death made her suddenly appreciate what she might be losing.'

She shivered for a moment, and in the darkness Lachlan took her hand. 'You OK?'

'It was a bit stressful…' She squeezed his hand. 'But I'm so grateful you were here—it was wonderful to have your support. It's hard to be dispassionate when your own family's involved and I could see how upset Mum was.'

'When you think something's going to end, it makes you look at things differently. When we had our little tiff I think I realised just how much I cared for you, Christa. I hated arguing with you, especially over nothing at all! And now,' he said teasingly, 'we were rudely interrupted an hour or two ago. Can we resume what we were doing—start over again?'

'If you like,' she said, a little breathlessly, and a flicker of elation rippled through her—almost triumph that perhaps she'd cracked that aversion of his to long-term involvement. She smiled, her cheeks dimpling. 'If you really want to…'

So much for good intentions, she thought wryly.

'Hello, there! Come on, Sleeping Beauty—time to rise and shine!'

From the depths of the cosy duvet pulled up

over her ears Christa heard a familiar deep voice. She pulled the duvet up further and pretended she hadn't heard, then there was a dirty chuckle and the duvet was rudely whipped from her.

'Don't do that!' she shrieked. 'It's freezing!'

Lachlan looked down at her, grinning impishly, holding a mug of tea in his hand. He was wearing boxer shorts and nothing else, slight stubble on his chin, thick hair ruffled. He looked dangerously sexy and incredibly hard to resist. Christa changed her mind about being cross that the duvet had been removed and stretched out provocatively on the bed, deliberately and mischievously tempting him.

'Why don't you get back in and warm me up again?' she suggested wickedly.

He groaned. 'God, don't tempt me. Like a flash I would! Only that might mean we'll be even later than we are already…'

Despite saying that, he sat down on the side of the bed and leant over her, running his hands lightly over her soft breasts and flat stomach. 'So beautiful,' he murmured.

'What did you say about the time?' said

Christa, drowsy with contentment, winding her arms round Lachlan's neck, pulling him towards her.

'Only that we've got about ten minutes to get to the surgery…'

'*What?* You can't be serious!' Christa pushed her tousled hair out of her eyes, squinted at his watch on the bedside table and gave a little shriek, trying to sit up with Lachlan still on top of her. 'Oh, my God—it's after eight-thirty. How are we going to explain that to everyone?'

'I haven't a notion—possibly that it was a very busy evening, attending an emergency?'

'But the whole evening?'

'True… Perhaps we were discussing the patient's case afterwards?'

Lachlan's eyes twinkled into hers and Christa threw a pillow at him. 'Funny sort of patient conference,' she said, giggling, then put her hand to her mouth. 'Oh, God! Bertie and Mum—I should have rung first thing to find out how things are.'

'I rang about an hour ago while you were snuggled abed, snoring your head off. Bertie's in CCU and stable and your mother came home soon after he was admitted—he was asleep anyway. So you see, babe, no need to worry about anything.'

'Thank God for that,' she said.

Lachlan smiled, tracing his finger down her neck and into her cleavage, loving the tousled look of her, the soft, creamy texture of her skin against the sheets.

'Hell, if only it wasn't a workday. What wouldn't I be doing now?' he said longingly. 'It's only my magnificent willpower that's stopping me having my wicked way with you…' He got up from the bed. 'Anyway, there's steaming-hot coffee on the hob and plenty of toast downstairs. You need something to keep you going after last night.' He grinned cheekily.

Last night! Christa's heart did a loop the loop as she thought about what had happened in the space of a few hours. It had been so horrible when they'd quarrelled but after a wonderful night together it seemed they had moved to something more than light-hearted fun.

He looked down at her very lovingly and traced

a finger down her neck. 'We could be doing this every night if you moved in with me…' he said softly. 'What about it? I don't like rattling around here by myself!'

A surge of joy rippled through her. At last he'd admitted that he felt much more for her than a casual dalliance! She laughed up at him. 'I thought we weren't into long-term pledges,' she teased.

'Surely we've gone beyond that now, sweetheart?' He brushed her lips with his. 'I know I have…'

And her heart nearly exploded with happiness. For the first time in many years the future looked wonderful. Her old friend Suzy Collins had been wrong about Lachlan!

She smiled at him. 'Perhaps that little disagreement was a good thing—it's made us realise how much we mean to each other. But I'm sorry I went over the top about it all.'

He stroked her cheek gently. 'Nothing wrong with being concerned about your parents,' he said rather sadly. 'I should have considered my own mother much more than I did.'

Christa smiled at him. 'She must have forgiven you. The fact that she left you Ardenleigh is proof of that,' she commented, sipping the refreshing tea Lachlan had brought her. She looked at him from under her eyelashes, her voice teasing. 'Supposing this scheme of yours doesn't materialise and you've not enough money to restore it?'

He went to the huge windows and pulled back the curtains so that the light flooded in, and gazed out at the wonderful view of the garden and woods and the bright sea beyond.

He turned round to face her and said simply, 'Then it may take longer than I thought, but if you're here to help me we can do it together.'

Christa lay back on the bed for a precious minute, smiling in tender reminiscence of the wonderful loving night she'd spent with Lachlan. How sweet it had been to nestle close to him on the sheepskin rug in front of the fire he'd lit in the beautiful drawing room. His strong face had looked down at her in the half-light as he'd gently undressed her in front of the flickering flames.

'This is what we were meant to do, sweetheart—forget the past and live our own lives!'

And later they had gone up to the bedroom with the old sagging bed and fallen asleep in each other's arms—and now he'd told her that he wanted to be with her all the time. Life was perfect!

'You've a huge backlog of patients,' grumbled Ginny to them both as they stood like recalcitrant schoolchildren in front of the two receptionists. 'The natives are getting restless.'

'Apologies,' said Lachlan with a charming smile at them both. 'If you knew what a night we've had!'

Christa stifled a giggle and the girls nodded sympathetically. 'Oh, yes—poor old Bertie Smith taken to hospital with a heart attack, wasn't it? You've had an e-mail from Coronary Care at St Luke's about him. You poor things, you must be exhausted!'

'Just a little,' remarked Lachlan lightly. 'So who's doing the clinic today?'

'Sarah's doing the BP clinic for the oldies, but the rep's cancelled his appointment.'

'Thank goodness for that,' remarked Christa, giving them all a sparkling smile. 'Now, let's get started, shall we?'

Ginny stared at Christa's retreating back. 'Well! She looks as if she's lost sixpence and found a pound,' she remarked to the room. 'I haven't seen her looking so cheery for ages!'

Alice glanced at Lachlan astutely. 'Are you taking anyone to the dance?' she asked cheekily.

'That would be telling.' Lachlan smiled, one finger tapping his nose, as he went out of the room.

'I'd love to know who he's taking!' said Alice in a stage whisper to Ginny when they were alone.

Ginny didn't believe in gossip. 'I've no idea who it is, Alice—that's his business,' she said loftily.

Alice took no notice. 'I bet you anything Christa and Lachlan are up to something! I mean, they came in together this morning and I'd swear to it that Christa came across the courtyard from the house. I didn't see her come down the road. And did you see the way Lachlan looked at her?'

'Nonsense, Alice! Anyway, they bought separate tickets for the dance—if they were going as a couple, surely he'd have just bought two. And if she did come from the house this morning, it was probably because she'd been discussing Bertie Smith's heart attack last night.'

Alice giggled. 'I'm sure he wasn't thinking of Bertie Smith's heart—just what his own heart was doing when he was near Christa!'

'Rubbish! What are you like?' said Ginny dismissively, but all the same there was a thoughtful look in her eyes as she went to the desk to deal with a patient.

CHAPTER TEN

CHRISTA RIFFLED THROUGH her wardrobe and threw the limited selection of evening wear she had onto the bed. Everything looked tired and dated. It was so long since she'd been anywhere glamorous that she'd forgotten what she had to wear!

She was beginning to panic about what she should wear to the dance in two weeks. She definitely didn't want to appear in the smart little black sheath dress she'd worn two years ago to the same event. It was the very one she'd worn the night Colin had so gallantly ditched her for someone else!

She threw it onto a pile of other clothes she had marked out for the charity shop and decided the only thing to do was to trust to luck and go shopping at the weekend in the little boutique in the village, and hope it would have something inspiring to wear. She wanted to look knock-out good for Lachlan!

Selina's was a busy little shop—the only dress shop for miles around—and was owned by Ginny's sister, a glamorous girl who had been a model in her younger days. She was a friend of Christa's, although Christa hadn't been in her shop for ages, because there'd been no occasion to dress up for.

'Hello, stranger!' Selina grinned. 'Can I guess you've come for something for the village dance?'

'I certainly have—the only possible thing I've got is two years old and I don't like it any more.'

'Well, long or short? I've some lovely maxi dresses in…' Selina gave Christa an assessing look. 'I think with your lovely creamy complexion and auburn hair, a soft apricot colour would suit you, and I've got the very thing.'

From the back room she brought out a dress and held it up to Christa. 'Wow!' she said. 'Put that on immediately before someone else nabs it! It's made for you.'

And even Christa had to admit that she looked good in it—a lovely column of the softest apricot satin that clung to her in all the right places and plunged at the back down to her waist, more modestly at the front.

'You don't think it looks a little…well, daring?' suggested Christa rather nervously. 'I mean, I'm hardly wearing anything at all at the back!'

'Rubbish! You're young and beautiful—wear it while you can. You'll have every male in the place salivating!'

There was only one male that Christa wanted to impress. She gave a little giggle at the thought of Lachlan's reaction. 'OK, Selina—you're a great saleswoman. I'll have it!'

She swung out of the shop happily. Next week she'd be in Lachlan's arms on the dance floor, and she could almost feel their bodies moving in harmony together to some impossibly romantic tune. Then she laughed to herself—it would more likely be a heavy metal number from the local group who thought they were in with a shout on *The X Factor*!

She hung the dress on the wardrobe door and

flicked a duster round the living room with the radio belting out something cheery on the Saturday morning show. She hummed to the music. Lachlan was going to call for her on his way back from a run along the beach, and then they were going on a bracing walk through the woods to a local waterfall. She couldn't have been happier.

The front doorbell rang, and as usual Titan bounded to the door, growling ferociously.

'Don't you know me yet, Titan?' asked Lachlan, bending down to stroke the little dog. 'You're going to be seeing a lot more of me in the future!'

He had on old shorts and a battered sweatshirt round his shoulders, and as usual Christa felt that flip of excitement when she saw him.

'I won't kiss you.' He grinned. 'I need a shower first—you make some coffee at Ardenleigh while I'm making myself presentable.'

They walked back to the big house and Christa filled the kettle with water while he went upstairs. She wandered over to the table where a pile of old photographs was scattered—Lachlan had evidently been sorting things out. Christa leafed through them. Many were of Isobel and her husband with Lachlan as a little boy, and then when he was older, his arm around his mother. They looked a devoted little group, young Lachlan laughing up at them, his parents' hands on his shoulders. It revealed a window of happiness in his life, and emphasised the poignancy of how it had all been smashed so irrevocably.

From those old snapshots it was obvious that he had adored his parents, and how doubly sad it was that he'd gone abroad, cut off all ties from those he'd loved. No wonder now that he needed to assuage his guilt by meeting Isobel's requests—only then could he feel a sense of release from his guilt.

Then the kettle boiled and she made the coffee and poured out two mugs.

'God, that smells good,' said Lachlan, coming into the kitchen. His dark thick hair was slicked down across his head, and he smelled clean and fresh. 'First things first,' he murmured, and his mouth found hers, pressing her body to his hungrily.

Christa leant against him for a moment, loving the feel of his hard body against hers, then said gently, 'Those are lovely photos of your family, Lachlan—I couldn't help seeing them.'

He smiled wryly. 'I'm glad I found them. Shows that once upon a time I had a happy family.'

'We're going to look forward, remember?' she remarked. 'Lots of good times to come!'

He leaned against the cupboards and took a sip from his mug, looking at her over the rim. 'I can't think of anything better,' he murmured.

He poured himself some more coffee and said casually, 'What makes things even more wonderful, sweetheart, is that you are just the girl my mother wanted me to marry!'

She laughed. 'You don't know that!'

'I certainly do...'

'But the last time you spoke to her I was nowhere around!' she protested. 'For all you know, I might be the last person she would want. I doubt very much that she—'

Lachlan put a hand up as if to stop her talking. 'Will you listen for a second? I absolutely know that that is what she wanted—for you and I to be together…'

'How do you know for certain?'

'Because I have it from the horse's mouth!'

Christa frowned. 'I don't believe you! Anyway, we will never know what she really wanted, will we?'

'I can prove it to you.'

He went to the little dresser in the kitchen and opened a drawer and pulled out a letter. He unfolded it and gave it to her.

'Read it!' he said simply.

Christa recognised the writing immediately—a letter in Isobel's distinctive hand. She looked up at Lachlan.

'This is a private letter, Lachlan, from your mother—I don't need to read it.'

'Read it!' he repeated.

She shrugged and scanned the closely written page, feeling her eyes welling up as Isobel's voice came loud and clear through her writing. '"To my beloved son, Lachlan, I wish I could speak these words directly to you, but in case that doesn't happen, here are a few things I wish to say…'"

Isobel went on to write how she could completely understand Lachlan's attitude when his parents had broken up and why he'd felt he had to get away, and blaming herself entirely for everything that had gone wrong between them. She told him how she would love him to have Ardenleigh, the house he'd grown up in, and hoped he'd find happiness in it as he had when he'd been young.

"'And I want you to get married, my darling son, and have a happy family life—and I know exactly who I would like you to get married to! Christa Lennox has worked with me for six years and I have grown to love her like a daughter. I believe she would be perfect for you. She is fun, intelligent, kind and beautiful. I think I know her very well now, and I can think of no one better than Christa to be my daughter-in-law! I would have been so happy to know she was your wife.'"

Christa stared at the paper in her hand and swallowed hard as Lachlan stood watching her.

'Well?' he said. 'Do you believe me now?'

There was silence for a few seconds then she took a deep breath. 'Of course I do,' she said quietly. She turned the letter over in her hand rather distractedly, then put it on the table and said slowly, 'I suppose that's why you're keen to keep our relationship going—to fulfil your mother's wishes.'

Lachlan's mouth dropped. '*What?* Surely you don't really think that?'

'It seems we are both being influenced by our mothers,' she said in a tight little voice. 'I thought you were going out with me on your own account, not because Isobel said you should.'

He stared at her aghast. 'Don't be a fool,' he said roughly. 'That has nothing to do with it. I'd want to be with you, whatever my mother thought.'

'Would you?' she said sadly.

Christa felt cold, almost sick with remorse—what a blundering idiot she was! It was staring her in the face. Lachlan Maguire might be taking her out because he fancied her, but he'd been motivated by guilt and determination to do what his mother had wanted. He didn't really want to get married—he'd said as much once or twice, even her old friend Suzy Collins had known it—but the voice of Isobel came over powerfully in that letter. Lachlan would never have proposed marriage—if that was what it was—if his mother had not requested he do so!

Her eyes sparked with anger. 'Frankly, I'll be damned if I'm just going to be the means of assuaging your guilt about your mother, Lachlan—just fulfilling Isobel's wishes. I want to be the centre of your world, not part of a list you've ticked off of your mother's wishes: have the house; join the practice; marry me!'

He looked at her in disbelief. 'Come on—this is crazy! I only wanted you to know how happy she would have been! You and she were so close…'

'And what? Until now it's just been a bit of fun, a happy lark, which I suppose I went along with because I wanted so much to believe that you really loved me on your own account. But I was totally wrong, wasn't I? I'm just part of an arranged marriage—only I didn't know about the arrangement!'

Christa had never seen Lachlan so angry. A pulse beat on his forehead and his face paled, making his blue eyes seem even bluer. 'I don't know what the hell you're talking about—honey, I couldn't love you more if I tried. What makes you think anything else?'

'Why didn't you tell me?'

'Does it matter? OK, I didn't tell you at first because I thought you would think precisely what you've just said—that I was just doing what my mother wished. But I believed that now you'd only be thrilled that it was what she had wanted…' He came closer to her, holding her gaze. 'Surely you know that now I want you to marry me anyway?'

She took a deep breath and closed her eyes, then said bitterly, 'I don't know what I believe any more, Lachlan.'

Then, before Lachlan could stop her, she'd opened the kitchen door and was running through the courtyard and down the road to the village, with Titan bounding beside her.

Her head was spinning with conflicting emotions—she'd fallen for Lachlan Maguire, she'd hoped he was falling for her too. But she was damned if she was just going to be the means of assuaging his guilt about his mother, just fulfilling his mother's wishes. She needed Lachlan to love her for herself alone, not because a voice from the grave had told him to! She reached her house and went in, slamming the door as hard as she could behind her. As far as she was concerned, she'd had it with romance!

Lachlan started after her, then gradually slowed down, watching her figure disappear into the distance. He shook his head in bewilderment.

'Well done, Maguire,' he muttered sarcastically to himself. 'You handled that very well—managed to make Christa feel really desired and needed.'

He drove his hands hard into his pockets in frustration. Why the hell had he shown her that letter now? He loved Christa, wanted to be with her always, wanted to show her that all men weren't feckless heartbreakers like that bloody man Colin, and all he'd succeeded in doing had been to make her feel she was just his mother's choice, not his. He'd been a complete and utter fool.

At first he had scorned his mother's wish that he should marry Christa. Now it seemed she was all that he wanted and more. After all these years of shunning close relationships, he'd found someone he loved and needed.

'I'm not going to let her go without a fight,' he told himself grimly. 'Somehow I'll get her back!'

It wasn't easy for Christa to maintain a natural atmosphere between the two of them at work that week. She took great care to keep her distance, and meetings were brisk and to the point. Often she would look across at Lachlan covertly, and then think her heart would break because he looked so wonderful. But she'd done the right thing, hadn't she? He didn't really love her—he'd grow tired of her, just as Colin had done, and find someone else. She had to remember her friend Suzy's warning.

No, there wouldn't be any happy-ever-after and

wedding bells. Lachlan Maguire wanted to settle down merely out of a sense of duty to his mother.

She took paperwork home with her rather than do it in the surgery after hours, as she used to do. She couldn't bear the thought of bumping into Lachlan when there was no one else there to dilute the meeting.

Towards the end of the week, while Christa and Lachlan were sorting out their mail, Alice said brightly, 'Looking forward to the dance? We've got a really big crowd coming this year.'

Christa felt, rather than saw, Lachlan glance towards her, then thought with spirit that she wasn't going to stay in because of her rift with Lachlan.

'Sure I am,' she said lightly. 'It'll be good fun!'

Lachlan flicked an intense glance at Christa. 'I can't wait,' he said grimly, 'I love dancing.'

Alice giggled. 'Well, I'm bagging you for a dance before you're killed in the rush!'

A tantalising picture formed in Christa's imagination of herself drifting across the floor with Lachlan, held close to his body, his cheek against hers, his heart beating close to hers… How wonderful that would have been, she thought wistfully, but now…

She couldn't avoid being alone with him altogether, of course. On the Friday before the dance Lachlan drove up beside her in the car park, and leaping out of the car barred her way as she tried to go up the ramp to the surgery.

'For God's sake, Christa, can't we talk to each other? This is totally ridiculous! If you won't answer my texts or e-mails then speak to me face to face! We are two adults after all.'

Christa shook her head, trying to ignore the effect that his powerful frame, so very close to her, was having on her libido. 'Lachlan, surely you don't expect me to keep seeing you when it's all about Isobel's wishes, not yours! A marriage based on that just wouldn't work!'

He seized her arm. 'You little fool, can't you see I love you? Nothing to do with that bloody letter or your damned uncle. Believe me, honey, when I made love to you I forgot all about any reservations I may have had to start with, or that you were a Lennox. Frankly, I couldn't give a toss—you are you, and that is all I care about.'

And for a moment perhaps she was tempted. There was something about the soft intensity of his voice, the look of yearning in his eyes that made her long to be held in his arms. And then she thought of her bitter experience before of a broken love affair. She swallowed hard, trying to suppress the tears that threatened to roll down her cheeks.

Several times she'd wondered if she should leave the practice and look for a job elsewhere, rather than endure this stilted relationship. Now she was sure she would have to do just that and try and start again. Her mother had Bertie and she didn't need her around any more—there was no reason to stay in the area.

She got into the car and drove off, leaving Lachlan alone in the car park.

Lachlan watched Christa go in despair, and yet he understood her reaction. He'd mishandled the whole situation and he just didn't know what to do next. He needed to talk to someone—someone with a bit of sense. He decided to ring John

Davies, his solicitor—at least he'd listen, even if he couldn't advise!

A girl with a pram was crossing the drive. She was thin and shabbily dressed and vaguely familiar. She looked up at Lachlan and gave a sudden smile.

'Hello, Doc!' she said. 'I had the baby!'

Preoccupied as he was, Lachlan didn't recognise her at first. She grinned at him.

'Don't remember me, do you? It's Lindsay Cooper. I came into the surgery a few weeks back…you sorted me out.'

'Of course, I do remember you, Lindsay. You're Greg's girl, aren't you?' Lachlan sighed inwardly—he had to show interest, however depressed he was. 'What did you have?'

'A little lad,' said Lindsay proudly. 'I was going to bring him in to show you…wanted you to know what we'd called him!'

'And what have you called him?'

'We've decided on Lachlan—that's your name, isn't it? You helped save Greg's life and you helped me.' She smiled shyly at him. 'You don't mind, do you?'

Lachlan was touched. 'I'm honoured, Lindsay. Let me see your little son.' He peered under the hood of the pram at the baby, rosy-cheeked and sleeping with a dusting of blond hair. 'He's beautiful—congratulations to both of you. How is Greg?'

'They say he'll be out of hospital soon, and social services have found us a little flat.'

'So things are going well, then?'

Lindsay's thin little face lit up. 'Yeah—couldn't be better! Will you let that other doc know—tell her thanks. If I'd had a girl I'd have called her Christa!'

'Yes. I'll tell her if I see her,' sighed Lachlan.

The village hall was an old square building situated at the edge of the village on a slight hill overlooking the sea. It had been dimly lit to make it look what was optimistically called 'atmospheric' by the committee of the annual charity dance. An attempt to make the place look festive had been provided by little paper lanterns hung across the ceiling, and a local DJ was testing the microphone, by intoning, 'One two, one two,' into it, his voice booming out over the hum of conversation.

The staff from the Ardenleigh Medical Practice were seated at a table in the corner, Alice sitting on the knee of her current boyfriend and Ginny next to her tubby little husband, Barry.

She should have been on top of the world, thought Christa sadly. Instead, she felt about as festive as a bear with a sore tooth, forcing herself to laugh at Ben's weak jokes and greeting all the locals with a smile.

It had been an ordeal to come, but she was determined that she was not going to do a rerun of her experience with Colin and opt out of everything when their romance had ended. Her heart might be broken yet again, but this time she was going to push it to the back of her mind, keep her life going, even though she felt on edge every time anyone fresh came into the hall, in case it was Lachlan Maguire. She half wanted him to come, to show him that she could do without him, and half hoped he wouldn't because she was afraid her heart would break when she saw him.

'You look fantastic, Christa—that apricot colour's just gorgeous,' said Sarah, the practice nurse. 'I wish I could wear something like that—the trouble is, with my figure I'm limited to things that hide it rather than show it!'

'You look great,' protested Christa. 'I feel a little self-conscious really—there isn't much room for manoeuvre in this…'

'You don't need to do much manoeuvring,' said Sarah drily. 'Just stand there and look fantastic!'

There were so many people there Christa knew—Richie from the gym, John Davies the solicitor, friends from her running group. Soon she would have to give in her notice to the practice and all these old friends would know that she was leaving. She took a deep swig of the cheap wine that was on offer and hoped it would help to deaden the pain she was feeling.

By now the disco was blasting away at full volume and Ginny and Barry were doing a very stylish quickstep, with much twirling and sidestepping. Alice and her boyfriend were swaying together with their arms around each other, their eyes closed, oblivious to the rest of the room. Christa leant against the wall and put the cool glass to her hot cheeks, an oppressive headache starting to throb behind her eyes. She closed them tiredly.

The voice in her ear was so familiar, deep and resonant. 'Christa, I'm glad you've come. I wasn't sure whether you'd make it or not. But we need to talk, *please*.'

Her eyes flew open, and her heart lurched when she saw Lachlan standing in front of her, looking ultra-cool in a cream shirt, open to the neck, and navy chinos.

For a second speech eluded her, then she said tightly, 'We can't talk here, Lachlan—not in a crowded dance hall.'

'Then let's go somewhere else.' His eyes wandered over her slim figure, the way her dress moulded to every curve and how the apricot colour enhanced her glowing skin. 'My God, Christa—I can't bear this,' he said roughly. 'You look quite…beautiful.' He hesitated and then said huskily, 'Please, let's have a dance together—just one.'

'That's not a good idea, Lachlan,' she said unsteadily. 'You…you don't need to have a duty dance with me.'

'For God's sake,' he said savagely.' His hand took her bare arm and she shivered, feeling the flickers of desire going through her like a hot knife through butter.

'If you don't trust me, if you really want us to part, think of it as a "last waltz". We can't end like this, with no communication at all!'

The words 'we can't end like this' echoed sadly in Christa's ears. She wanted him, oh, how she wanted him, longed for everything to be as it had been before when she'd thought he loved her for herself alone… Just one more time, then. She offered no resistance when he put his arm around her waist and pressed her body fiercely to his.

It was a kind of torture, reminding her of their lovemaking only a few days ago, when his body had locked with hers and they had been as one. He put his cheek to hers and she could smell the scent of soap on him, the slight roughness of his chin, feel his legs against hers as they moved in unison to the beat of the music.

It was as if they were welded together—and it was wonderful and terrible at the same time. Would this really be the last time she would ever be so close to him, ever feel his breath on her face, his lips tracing a trail of little kisses down her neck?

'Stop it!' she whispered fiercely in his ear. 'I don't want to do this…it's not fair! People will see us and get the wrong idea!'

'Rubbish, the lights are too low for anyone to see anything.' He smiled, his arm tightening around her.

God, how beautiful she felt against him, thought Lachlan, an aching sadness somewhere around his heart. Her hair had a faint fresh smell, her body felt sexy and curvy under her silk dress, and he felt an indescribable longing for her. He'd been a bungling idiot, not realising how bruised and damaged she'd been after her experience with Colin Maitland. He looked down at her, seeing her long lashes lying against the curve of her cheek.

'Christa…Christa, darling, give me a chance to explain. Don't let us part like this.'

With a great effort she pulled away from him, suddenly unable to bear the paradox of being so close to him physically yet so distant from him in other ways.

'There's nothing to explain,' she said lightly. 'No hard feelings at all. And now, if you don't mind, I want to sit down.'

She sat rigidly in the chair, tossing back the rest of her wine, and he sat next to her—silence between them. Then eventually Lachlan got up and walked out of the room.

'Ah! Christa!' said a jolly voice. 'How about a turn on the floor? I'm not much good, but if you can put up with me?'

John Davies, the solicitor, was beaming down at her. She knew him quite well, having had to deal with him when Isobel had died. She smiled and jumped up, glad to take her mind off Lachlan.

They started off round the floor, John taking everything rather slowly and carefully and holding her as if she was made of delicate china.

Eventually he began to relax and said jovially,

'So what do you think of Lachlan's idea of putting Ardenleigh on the market?'

Christa stiffened with surprise and stopped moving, causing them both to stumble. 'Put Ardenleigh on the market?' she repeated in amazement. 'When did he tell you that?'

John looked flustered. 'Oh, dear. That was most indiscreet and unprofessional of me. I really thought you knew. He came to see me late this morning.'

'But…why does he want to sell it? I thought… I thought Isobel wanted him to have it?''

John looked embarrassed. 'You'll have to ask him the reason, my dear. I shouldn't have mentioned it at all.'

She stopped dancing again and looked imploringly at John. 'It…it's really important that I know just why he wants to sell Ardenleigh. I thought he loved the place and, of course, wanted to fulfil his mother's wishes.'

John shook his head and smiled. 'Christa, I'm not going to say any more. Lachlan's here—you go and ask him!'

Christa bit her lip. 'Oh, dear, the thing is, we've

had a bit of a falling out…I don't know that he would feel like telling me.'

The elderly man looked at her shrewdly and laughed. 'Then go and make it up with him. I know this much—he adores you. I know he can't stop talking about you. That much I am allowed to say. Said he wished he'd met you ages ago!'

'Did he say that?' she said in a small voice.

John Davies smiled. 'He certainly did.' He looked at her, suddenly concerned by the expression on her face. 'Is something wrong, Christa?'

'I think, John, I've been very, very silly… Do you mind if I go and find Lachlan? I need to say something to him.'

'Of course, my dear. I'll see you later.' John gave a little bow and wandered off to the bar.

Was she too late? Had Lachlan gone home? Whatever happened, she had to see him that evening, tell him how very, very wrong she'd been. She'd been an impetuous fool, jumping to completely the wrong conclusions.

She dashed outside, hardly noticing as the cold air hit her body. By the wall of the car park stood a solitary figure, gazing out over the moonlit sea, watching the beam on the lighthouse across the firth swing over the water every minute or two.

How lonely and forlorn Lachlan looked in that setting. He'd had sadness in his life, admitted he made mistakes, and she had thrown everything he'd said back in his face.

Would he take her back, give them another chance? She ran up to him and touched his arm. 'Lachlan…' she said breathlessly. 'Lachlan, perhaps you were right. We need to talk…'

He whipped round with a start. 'What the…? Christa? I didn't expect to see you again tonight.'

'I've been such a fool. I've been speaking to John Davies. He told me you want to sell Ardenleigh! Is that true?'

His amazing blue eyes looked sadly down at her. 'I began to realise that without you it didn't matter a toss where I lived—and neither do I want to stay at the practice if I'm not with you.'

'But it's what your mother wanted. I thought you would do anything to keep it—sell the land for money…'

'She wouldn't want me to be unhappy, I'm sure.'

Christa's eyes filled with tears and put her hands on his shoulders. 'Don't say that, Lachlan—and don't leave me. I want you to stay.' She put her arms around his waist, looking up into his eyes, and said in a small voice, 'Darling Lachlan—I want you to forgive me. I've been such an idiot.'

He shrugged, his face shadowed in the moonlight. 'But no matter what I say, you don't seem to believe that I love you.'

'I was wrong,' she whispered, biting her lip. 'John Davies made it clear to me that you loved me, and I don't think I could bear it if you left…'

A flicker of amusement passed over Lachlan's face. 'So you're prepared to believe what John Davies says, even if you didn't believe me!'

She smiled up at him. 'Well, he is a solicitor…'

It was as if Lachlan was struck dumb for a moment, then he threw back his head and laughed. 'Good God. Haven't I demonstrated it most graphically?'

'Yes, you have, Lachlan,' said Christa meekly.

He encircled her with his arm and hugged her to him, cradling her head against his chest, a beaming smile on his face.

'Is this true, Christa? You finally believe me?'

She nodded, unable to speak.

Lachlan grinned a cheeky schoolboy grin. 'I didn't realise I was going out with an idiot, but it looks as if I am! I owe John Davies a lot!'

In sheer happiness he took her hands and whirled her round, then caught her in his arms.

'Perhaps now we can get on with the rest of our lives, my love. We'll make a fresh start and buy a new home with our stamp on it—not with the ghosts of previous generations at our backs.'

Lachlan wiped away a tear that rolled down Christa's face and smiled. 'Are you beginning to regret coming back to me?'

'It…it's because I'm so happy,' she gulped. 'A few minutes ago I was beyond sad, and now I just can't describe how I feel!'

'I know one thing, you're freezing,' he whispered. 'And I know a very good way to warm you up, and it's even better than dancing. Let's go back to your house and I'll show you!'

He took her hand and they left the sound of the dancing behind them.

EPILOGUE

SPRING HAD COME late to Errin Bridge, but now, looking down the valley from the top of Errin Hill, one could see the fresh green mist of new leaves on the trees and a scattering of daffodils over the village green.

So much had happened in six months, thought Christa, looking around with pride at the old farmhouse that she and Lachlan had just bought. It was only small and a far cry from the grandeur and space of Ardenleigh, but it nestled at the side of the hill and commanded the most beautiful views of the countryside and the little village below. Ardenleigh had been sold and there were plans to make it into a retirement home—something that was desperately needed in the area.

In a few minutes guests for their house-warming party would be arriving, and Christa went into the living room and looked around doubtfully, wondering if all their guests would be able to fit into it!

Lachlan came in from the back, where a little copse of trees grew, and threw some logs on the fire—everywhere looked cosy and neat. He put his arms around her and nuzzled her neck.

'Glad we moved here, darling, and didn't stay at Ardenleigh?' he murmured.

She looked at him with a dimpled smile. 'This could be too small in a year or two—but of course I love it here!' she replied.

'Before everyone arrives, I've something for you, actually...a kind of moving-in present!'

'I like the sound of that!' She smiled. 'What is it?'

'Something to wear...but a little more permanent than a dress!'

Lachlan pulled a little box out of his pocket and gave it to her. 'Open it quickly before all our friends come,' he said.

She opened the lid and stared at the sparkling diamond ring that nestled in the white satin box, and then looked up at him in speechless amazement, her lovely eyes wide with disbelief.

He watched her with a wry smile. 'Well?' he demanded. 'Do you like it or not?'

'Oh, Lachlan...' she murmured. 'Of course I like it...it's beautiful!'

He tilted her chin towards him and his eyes were tender and warm. 'I think we've waited long enough for this, sweetheart. Will you marry me? It'll make me the happiest man on the earth if you will!'

A startled silence and then Christa gave a burst of laughter. 'And this from the man who said marriage wasn't for him!' she teased. 'What's brought this on?'

'After six months living together I thought you'd realise by now that my mother's wishes have nothing to do with us getting married! Now we're in our new home, starting a new life, it seems the perfect time. What do you say, sweetheart—ready for the final leap?'

She put up a hand and stroked his wonderful face. Strange to think that not so long ago she'd been in the depths of despair, love and marriage seemingly a far-off dream.

'Of course I'll marry you!' she said.

And he slipped the ring onto her finger. 'To love and to cherish,' he murmured softly.

Then the guests began arriving and they wondered at first why the hostess was laughing and crying at the same time.

* * * * *

Mills & Boon® Large Print Medical

December

200 HARLEY STREET: THE SOLDIER PRINCE	Kate Hardy
200 HARLEY STREET: THE ENIGMATIC SURGEON	Annie Claydon
A FATHER FOR HER BABY	Sue MacKay
THE MIDWIFE'S SON	Sue MacKay
BACK IN HER HUSBAND'S ARMS	Susanne Hampton
WEDDING AT SUNDAY CREEK	Leah Martyn

January

200 HARLEY STREET: THE SHAMELESS MAVERICK	Louisa George
200 HARLEY STREET: THE TORTURED HERO	Amy Andrews
A HOME FOR THE HOT-SHOT DOC	Dianne Drake
A DOCTOR'S CONFESSION	Dianne Drake
THE ACCIDENTAL DADDY	Meredith Webber
PREGNANT WITH THE SOLDIER'S SON	Amy Ruttan

February

TEMPTED BY HER BOSS	Scarlet Wilson
HIS GIRL FROM NOWHERE	Tina Beckett
FALLING FOR DR DIMITRIOU	Anne Fraser
RETURN OF DR IRRESISTIBLE	Amalie Berlin
DARING TO DATE HER BOSS	Joanna Neil
A DOCTOR TO HEAL HER HEART	Annie Claydon

1114 LP 1P Medical